PARADE

PARADE

BY EMILIANA HELFELD

Enjoy the Pastries!

This is a work of fiction. Names, characters, places, and incidents either are the product of the author's imagination or are used fictitiously. Any resemblance to actual persons, living or dead, events, or locales is entirely coincidental.

Copyright © 2021 by Emiliana Helfeld

All rights reserved. No part of this book may be reproduced or used in any manner without written permission of the copyright owner except for the use of quotations in a book review.

Second paperback edition February 2021

Book design by Kira Freed
Cover art by Amalia Russiello

ISBN 9798704435716

For my Jack, curled inside a distant summer

ONE

Perfect serendipity—the way it all was. We were lovers crossed by stars, erotic sinners splattered in oil paint. Dusk crept into our bones, as nostalgic and mysterious as a black sky, and the sun hazed a mosaic of stained glass onto the train platform. A sliver of the coming night twinkled far down the tracks. It was August, and the humidity stuck to you like a glistening second skin. The misery carved into people's faces as they grimaced and wiped away the coatings above their brows, pulling bandanas across their necks, desperately trying to dry themselves in the wet air. And the sun—God, the sun. It brushed across these people and their miserable faces, casting the golden pale of late summer upon everything it touched, and leaving everything else in black shadow. There would be nothing more beautiful than this, the most beautiful day that ever was.

My woman stood there across the platform, so striking that the solar film couldn't dull her or bleach her into the surrounding summer evening. Golden and dark-featured, she was colored and detailed like a Faberge egg. Her dark, thick hair billowed behind her in a cloud of rich curls, each strand whistling between the others like an orchestra—her hair a soft parade. Between those rhythmic curtains rested a face all pointed and plump. Eyes speckled in yellow flakes and sparkling from their green abyss, just like a glittering sidewalk on a sun-flushed day. And she was flushed, too, pink and erotic, with her cheeks rosed, touched by the sun. Those speckled cheeks, dusted with faint freckles, were redolent of a honeybee. In fact, she looked just like a honeybee covered in pollen, standing there and impregnating flowers. Raspberry nectar filled her lips, fruit-stained as if she had sat all day in an orchard, gorging on nectarines. She looked delicious, my woman, like a bowl of ripe peaches drizzled in forest honey.

From across the tracks, I called out to her in my bird song, "Hey! HEY!" waving my arms wildly in the air, and she looked at me with her yellow-striped face, then quickly looked away. Couldn't she recognize me through those compound eyes? Arms gesticulating, I jumped up and down—anything to catch the eye of my lover. Everyone looked at me, except her. Instead, she hurried farther down the platform, away from me. *She didn't recognize me.* I sprinted toward the stairs to join her on the other side and caress her hands, covered in corbiculae, still bright and sticky with pollen.

I tore down the stairs and crossed under the tracks to the opposite side. Ascending there, I fluffed up my plumage and called out to her in my bird song. She frowned as I got closer —visibly agitated, all buzzing and hostile. Never had I seen her like this, or ever outside of the hive. She, this buzzing thing, and I a fat sparrow bird, ready to feast on those ripe lips she kept dripping in honey. Could this be a lover's quarrel? I grabbed her hands violently, and her thousand-lensed eyes went wide and fearful. She wrenched them back, and she was fully human again as she ran down the platform and all the way down the stairs. I heard the spin of the turnstile as she flew out, still ruffled and buzzing, surely headed toward the hive. Confused, I shook my head, ignoring the angry glares from pedestrians. It had to be the mirage of an intolerable late sun, forcing us into faces we normally didn't wear—mine, one my woman couldn't recognize. I'd thought she only came out at night, long after the sun had fallen from the sky, pulling with it the day. The sun was sinking low now, night falling into place behind it. I decided to head to her hive, where, certainly, I'd see my woman, and show her my true face that only the black sky could reveal.

She was the queen of the colony, and I just a blue-collared worker, caressing her regality with my vibrissae. Once, I had been royalty, too, thriving in a jungle of capitalism, in a kill or be killed corporate system that speared me through the heart. Now, I survived on odd jobs for my uncle and managed to make just enough to fund my trips to the Theater.

Metal ground against metal in a wretched shriek as the train came screaming up the tracks. Sharp, creaking, and squealing. I pressed my palms into my ears. Faces peered from the train's belly, the faces and the machine together condemned to the propulsion of endless time, with the fixed, unmoving track forever stuck in its only two directions. I would be no victim to this passage of reviled chronology, this march to death. I rushed down the same stairs she had, following that furious, bee-faced woman. As the train cars came whistling to a smokey, achingly slow halt, I slinked through the turnstile, following the trail of glittering pollen my woman had left behind.

TWO

Intoxicated by the honey scent that lingered on my fingertips, I grinned a full smile, broad and bursting with elation. I screamed in laughter and ignored the frightened looks and scowls from people I passed on the street. I stretched my arms over my head. *Thank God I'm alive!* I felt ripe—ripe as my woman's lips.

Few other people walked around me, but the street itself hummed with the living. Each car that passed pushed the sound waves to either side, only for those seconds, before they would SNAP back into place, continuing their hypnotic rhythm.

I hummed, too, like a comet that lacked arching grace. I jittered down the street and everyone I passed started to vaporize into the orange, sunset atmosphere. The sidewalk kept glittering as they vanished, unperturbed. Glorious solitude. I felt freedom from their judgment, their senseless, social regulations. I cheered every time someone puffed up into smoke, happy that they were gone and happy it hadn't been me instead.

The sidewalk undulating in front of me, I strutted down a promenade of clacking roller coaster tracks. I passed alley after alley in this filthy, desecrated city, each one more sun-drenched than the last. I stopped and stared into every exquisite backstreet. Each contained an entire forest, broad as the space between two buildings but infinitely deep and vast, with trees swallowing the horizon whole. They were evidence of a before world, artifacts carved out from the concrete jungle, of a slow, brimming, primordial life. From the edge of the crumbling concrete, I peered into the years before the settlement, before development, before civilization had recognized capitalism as its new god.

The clouds parted and poured prisms of light into each alley like Heaven emptying its contents back into the earthly world, forgotten ghosts returning to an equally forgotten time. I gazed into these overgrown alleys, creaking with ever-proliferating life. Within each passage grew a cloud of birds, all fluttering and prim. Leading the swell was the hoopoe drum major, with his elaborate feather shako, marching knee to chest and beating his baton against his full, extended breast. There were the heather falcon color guards, intense and moving proudly in allegiance to nothing in particular, as blind as nationalism itself. The finches crooned into their flutes while the fregatidae murmured into the mellophones, and the treeswifts and true swifts alike wailed into the clarinets like a whistling train. Birds everywhere, swooping in thick trills of pastels, magenta, and ruby. Plumb jays, honeyguides, tangerine- and tan-tinted finches, and beautiful birds of paradise, all coffee- and saffron-hued. Even middling yard birds preened their finery alongside birds painted blue as lapis lazuli. Had I not gotten lost in these backstreets, I would never have seen those passiongales swelling in a cirrus sea against the gilded amber skies, this marching band of wildfowl, an eccentric parade of music and plume.

Some of these alleys were so pregnant with fruiting groves, I wondered if my woman sat here to feast and thus stained her lips so plumb. The orange harvests brimmed so full, and the sky was barely visible from under those native trees. I looked upon a firmament made entirely out of citrus fruit. These thick forests were spotted with bevies of deer, their giant, shy eyes seeking the sweet summer grass through curls of lacing lilacs. Their fragile, thin legs quietly brushed through gossamer wreaths of spiderwebs and dainty pools of rainfall. Long-necked and gentle, they too stopped and took in the entire splendor of the earth contained in these simple paradises.

As night continued to overtake the day, the animals began to settle themselves for sleep. Birds settled together in pairs, their bodies resting together like warm, feathered hearts. Curled up safe in the brush, there slept the deer. Even the orange trees drooped comfortably, resting from their long day of photosynthesis. Night fell and the world fell blue. The fireflies stuck out like falling diamonds.

I smirked to myself, ready to transform just as the world had into night.

THREE

Women come into the world on a schedule. In the mornings, there are the Day Beauties; the women who open like morning glories, unfolding at dawn, radiant for the day. Their smooth faces soft like a milk bath, cheeks rouged as if pulled in a pinch, their innocent lips pale from sleep. Day Beauties' do not fade; they are permanent and often contrived, appeasing a standard narrative, like whitewashed marble statues in Rome. Maybe their glittering eyes sit unassumingly in the face. Or their informal dress, fitted at the waist, dances and sings all down their hips and far past their thighs, modestly. In the night, they wash the chemical art from their faces and bathe in lavender-scented waters. Pinning their hair up, they coat themselves in emollient, and then, letting their hair cascade like a flight of stairs, they brush a mahogany shine into their tresses. Wrapped up into a cocoon of cotton, they sleep under the blue glow of the moon (under which we are all shape-shifters). Their subconscious drifts away from all of the proper things that young ladies should dream about, Prince Charmings and wedding gowns. Their true, salacious desires create a single line of connection, a mutual consciousness, shared with the women of the underworld.

When the sun sets and all these Day Beauties are asleep, the night opens with neon lights and the bells of shot glasses. Now, the Night Beauties wake up from their sunset naps and the Days have long settled. They emerge like nightingales during a twilight spring. They clatter in their six-inch platform heels, like hooved horses, and just as proud and majestic. Their sun-starved complexions are vibrant with artificial color—pearl eyeshadows blended right below the brow bone, highlighting black daggers of eyebrows, and with those fresh, stained lips red as sin. Working women in love with themselves, in love with money and the night. They dip their long, lithe legs into champagne bubble baths, fluttering their feet into expensive ponds of rosé. Their aroma is sweet and expensive, their bodies peppered with freckles of glitter. Their hair, wild and full, like the feathers of a Las Vegas showgirl, and they, too, fluff up their plumage and swell their full breasts like crimson thrusts in heat.

Yes, these Night Beauties were the women claiming my allegiance, whom I only ever saw after the heat of sundown had passed. Of course, the Day girls were pretty, but they were too innocent, too domesticized, and too un-ripened by the world.

God, these Night girls, these ruthless call girls. During their afternoon-formed mornings, they sit at great dining tables that have blossomed with feasts. They are served elaborate *charcuterie*—plattered on silver, of course—featuring expensive *pâté* richer than butter, *Iberico* cuts that melt like ice cream on the tongue, *prosciutto* thinner than silk threads, and even that black, gruesome *bresaola*. The platters are lined with huge stems of amethyst grapes, the fruit so bursting and full that your mouth aches for you to pop them. Seemingly an orchard-full of August peaches and just-September apples sit in thrones of wicker. Boards of thick filet mignon rest rare in pools of their own blood. Saucers of caviar flow like billows of fabric all down the table, glowing in jewel tones of warm golds and punchy orange, onyx, and ruby red. Huge, vermillion-tinted lobsters lay prostrate in pools of *beurre d'Echiré*, their open spines herbed to absolute perfection. Wheels of pungent, almost repugnant, brie twirl around baskets full of sweet breads and decadent pastries. Raspberry cakes, dressed in sable chocolate shells, glisten with sweet cream florets. Boxes of truffles and saffron are scattered about the table, as if placed only for their opulence.

The girls sit at these feasts fit for the Last Supper, and take one mousy bite out of each delicacy, a slight sip of champagne following each peck to cleanse their pallets. They sit in great armchairs, their meals supine in front of them, and they recline. Oh, how they recline, and their disciples recline with them, tucking their checkbooks back into their breast pockets. After they have taken their nibbles, just to say that they have dined in the very crook of luxury, they rise and begin their late-set days. What is left of the untouched spread is thrown away, and a brand new feast is curated for the next late morning, it being a meal as luxurious and wasteful as the one before. At nightfall, the women feast again, but this time on the pockets of men, their patrons who worship them.

Those male drones, so innately driven by God or by nature to spend their entire lives seeking out pussy. Their sole decided purpose in this meaningless life is to fuck these worker bees, each purporting herself to be the Queen. These contemptible-looking flowers sit back in their silk suits, watching their money make itself, legs spread lewdly, beckoning a honeybee between them. Yes, these night women, by all appearances, and through the pink smoke screens they masquerade behind, seem to be queens of their own colonies. However, their exceptional and lascivious lives require an enormous amount of work. They search the same fields, day in and day out, for the most lavish, the richest, or most ostentatious flowers from which to finesse that luxurious pollen. And then these worker bees, wings fatigued from long nights, fly back to their hive, legs glistening in pollen that will become dark, rich honey.

Deep within the failed industrial sector, far on the west side of town, was the great wax nest molded into a gap in the abandoned cityscape. It sat there for decades; Christ, I remember walking past it as a kid, and that distinctive humming…my shoes would be sticky with honey. My friends and I would hurl insults at the sight of the women in their lewd fur coats, and the men going in to see the *titty show*.

Back in those days, we used to be able to sneak up the fire escape that let out in the alley. On summer nights, we would push past the wild, overgrown weeds—massive, untended, flowering bushes. The fire escape dangled high above the ground, and it took many years until we had grown tall enough to reach it. Only the biggest and strongest of us could make it up the ladder. We crept up the steps and peered into a large-paned window. It opened into the women's lounge adjacent to the dressing room. Cigarette butts lay discarded on the sill, which we brushed aside as we gripped it in anticipation of seeing uncovered women's bodies.

Inside, women lay on loveseats in satin robes, flipping through magazines, chatting, or fixing an eyelash while waiting for the next garish customer to come in blossoming with cash, making it worth their while to get up off the sofa. We stared at these women doing normal things, being completely average despite their beauty, and we would hope—pray, wish upon a star—that we might catch a glimpse of a nipple or the fields between a pair of legs. More often than not, one of them would glance at the window and catch us ogling, open-mouthed. Then the shoes, the insults, and the curses would come flying. They'd run up to the window buzzing furiously—just like my woman. Quickly, we would fly back down the fire escape, jump to the ground below, and run for our lives, tails between our legs. With the increasing distance, our panic would subside, and we would burst into fits of laughter, each boy swearing they hadn't been afraid.

Our budding masculinity; a feat of strength, followed by our invasion of this private female world. Women were a species we were so unfamiliar with. We proved ourselves powerful, and any boy who was too short, too weak, or too afraid to make it up the fire escape was a *pussy*. But our understanding of all that we knew to be manhood changed the night we met Lilith, the true Hive Queen.

We were each fifteen or sixteen, all pimpled and gross. There we stood, perched at the windowsill, eyes like dinner plates as one woman crossed and uncrossed her legs. We held our breath, waiting for her to open her legs wide enough so we could see between them. We were a perverted sight of puberty, us boys, mouths agape and drooling.

Suddenly, we heard shouting from below–loud, venomous, contemptuous shouting.

"Get the fuck off my goddamn fire escape!"

Our necks twisted toward the ground as every woman in the lounge turned to look at us. The voice continued, *"You goddamn cocksuckers, get off my goddamn fire escape before I come up there and throw you the fuck off!"* The longer the voice carried on for, the more pairs of glittering, smoky, thick-lashed eyes came into view from beyond the window. They were laughing at us; those goddamned hookers were laughing at *us*.

We had been caught before, but now we weren't caught; we had been captured. Our only way out was the low-hanging mouth of the fire escape from where this contemptuous voice was erupting. There were so many of us, but we had lost all of the audacity that had drawn us to this window in the first place. Shame spread across my face. A six-inch stiletto shoe to the face was to be expected, but our pubescent pride offered no defense for ridicule.

The voice got louder and louder, the farther we descended. Slowly, shamefully, heads hung low, we came down the fire escape, and it continued.

"Stupid child-pigs. Boys, men, it doesn't matter, you all hang out on the short end of civilized."

As we got lower, we could see a body belonging to this wicked, demanding, cogent voice. It was just some woman—some little woman.

The woman screamed in her vile way. Slender-hipped, she'd have been short if it hadn't been for the massive, gold stilettos strapped all around her ankles and halfway up her calves. Her skintight dress had to have been painted on. It came around her breasts, which were practically spilling out of the halter opening. Diamonds sparkled from her lithe neck. Earrings dangled to her collarbone, twinkling with sound at every slight movement. Her wrists jangled like church bells calling at noon. Her hair swung high in a ponytail. Long and obsidian, it shined despite the darkness of night. She stood there with hands on her hips, a fine dust of pollen falling all around her.

Her pretty face contorted in anger and she bared her teeth—growling as, one by one, we jumped off the fire escape onto the ground, our steps crunching with jeweled leaves. Above us, the women had taken our place on the fire escape. They stood in their satin robes, chatty and smirking. The flutter of their eyelashes shed more glitter and pollen onto our shoulders. The Night women called down to this authoritative voice, "Give it to 'em, Lilith!", and the woman, Lilith, shot back a slick smile, then narrowed her eyes towards us.

Standing in front of us, she crooned, "Get down on your knees, all of you." We shifted our eyes back and forth around our group of hairy-handed perverts, our faces furrowed in uncertainty. None of us moved, and this infuriated Lilith. This time, she barked, "I caught your hands in the cookie jar, NOW GET DOWN ON YOUR GODDAMN KNEES!" Shyly, the most unsure I know I've ever been, I began to kneel. My face still burned red, my pride completely decimated, and my solitary comfort was the shuffling sounds of my friends around me, also dropping to their knees.

Lilith looked pleased. She walked right up to our line of miserable, humiliated boys and paced like a drill sergeant. With each turn on her stiletto heel, I caught a glimpse of an angel wing tattooed on each shoulder. Ironic for this demon straight from the inferno.

Standing squarely in front of us now, she made her next demand.

"Turn out your pockets and throw your money on the ground in front of you."

We all began to murmur in protest. We had no money. A few of us worked summer jobs, but for the most part, we walked around with the pocket change we could scrounge from our parents.

Lilith wasn't having any of it. Suddenly, her manicured fingers gripped a braided whip. I hadn't seen her reach for it, and I hadn't noticed it before; it seemed to materialize from thin air. The whip was crafted out of long, thin, black leather. She kept the handle in her right hand and pulled the tail taught in her left.

"There are no free shows here," she crooned. "You ate the steak; now, it's time to pay up."

We did not move.

She kicked her right leg out for leverage and threw all her might into her right hand, cracking that whip into the air above her like Zeus releasing a huge crack of thunder. Everything in my body clenched. All of us thrust our hands into the pockets of our blue denim jeans and threw the contents out onto the mixture of dirt and gravel that made up the alley's ground. In front of us lay a bunch of crumpled dollars, keys, lighters, cigarettes, a pack of gum, and a condom. Five or six of us kneeled there, and we couldn't have scrounged together a solid twenty bucks.

I expected Lilith to laugh, to ridicule us further. She didn't crack a smile. She stoically marched past each of us and collected every shitty dollar bill. She counted it up and declared, "You boys have a problem here."

God, how I wanted to get up and run home, away from this humiliation.

"You're all seriously short. The show inside the Theater starts at $250 per half-hour. You little voyeurs were up looking in the private quarters, and I'd say that's worth even more."

Lilith cracked the whip again, this time right over *our* heads, and we all flinched as if we were the many dying legs of a twitching beetle.

"All of you will return here on each of the next seven nights, and you will make a ritual payment to me in my office. Do you understand me? Your debt will be paid one way or another."

We all nodded at her words, none of us with any intention of actually coming anywhere near that place ever again.

She turned on her heel and tilted her chin down. "You're dismissed," she crooned slyly, over her shoulder.

We all leapt to our feet and scurried past, our tails between our legs.

"Maybe when your balls come in, you can watch the real show—the front door is around that corner." Pointing towards the street, she giggled to herself.

Above us, the crowd of women roared with laughter, their pollen falling down all around us like snowfall. We all burned with shame except for my friend, John, whose face had reddened with anger. He spun around to face Lilith, who now stood several yards away, and said, "Those girls are just whores! Everyone sees them naked anyway, so why does it matter if we got a peek, too?!"

Silence. Every eye in that alley was on Lilith, and even the smallest, unseen creatures held their breath in anticipation of her reaction. Lilith stood there, eyes closed, stoic. We stood several feet behind John, willing him to shut up and willing ourselves to turn around and run while we still could.

CRACK.

In a seemingly impossible feat of speed and precision, Lilith had swung her whip over her head and struck it down upon John. Before our unbelieving eyes, John lost three-fourths of his stature, and his furious red visage mellowed to a porcine pink. His ears migrated to the top of his head, where they protruded like moth wings. This four-legged thing, his nose extended into a snout, had beady eyes set far back into his face. Squealing and bucking, he crashed against garbage cans and brick walls, stomping his cloven feet against gravel in protest of his new, unwelcomed form. We dodged his barnyard charging, wailing at his unclean flesh. Lilith stood with her arms crossed, smiling. The women above gasped for air in between raucous laughter. An oinking John stampeded out the alley, and the rest of us sprinted after him screaming his name, willing him to let us catch up.

"Consent my darling! The difference is consent!"

Eventually, John ran himself fully human again. I went home and immediately threw the porno magazines I'd had hidden under my mattress into the garbage—well, into the garbage of the husband and wife who lived next door. Late in the night, I woke up to her shrieks and his indolent excuses. Their aluminum can clattered as she tore the glossy pages to shreds. As I drifted back to sleep, I prayed silently, thanking God for delivering me from Lilith, and vowing to respect and honor women, to stay out of their private worlds, to bury my desires, and to stay away from whores.

Women, those pure, fragile flowers as I saw them; and our duty as men to protect and honor that purity represented our respect for the feminine. My father had always said this: *You got to avoid a woman that flaunts her sexuality, the promiscuous ones. They have no respect for themselves, so why should you?* Red-blooded men loved respectable women and whistled at the rest.

Jesus, if my dad could see me now.

As we got older and matured, the gazes of my childhood friends shifted, moving higher and higher up the shortest skirts.

My gaze remained much lower—low enough to catch sight of Eva's low-slung sandals. When I looked up, I noticed her unassuming clothes and her modest neckline, but looking into her face was like looking into an artist's palette. A docile woman, though we had our young, wild days. She was the one I thought I would love forever.

Eva was far from my mind as I walked up to the Theater now, searching for my woman. I heard the buzzing even before I made out its haunting glow. Its massive Roman pillars came into view. Blue, artificial light bathed the building's front, offering an ethereal touch amongst a very gaudy red-light district. Men droned around outside, either unashamed to be seen or unable to muster up the courage to go inside. I remember my palpable hesitation the first time I found myself covered in that neon blue light, when I was finally old enough to enter. The building only had one window out front; it stood out dimly, illuminated against the cast of the night. The true, reigning Hive Queen, Ms. Lilith, sat up there in her office, running her manicured fingers through hundreds of thousands of dollars' worth of small bills, pollen dusting to the ground as she rustled through the cash. She had long ago quit turning tricks, and now she spent her days reaping the benefits of her own little worker bees, all buzzing about and building up her waxy honey hive. The fields were full; there had never been a shortage of drones.

I walked in—head high, chest full—and a familiar world greeted me. The Theater was filled with clouds of night-blooming jasmine, and illuminated with a transparent purple glow, the source of which was a continuous mystery. Women floated past me, their long, iridescent legs fanning out to make each graceful step like they were a procession of flamingos. The women sighed at me lustfully, blowing kisses and caressing the crook of my neck with fingers that brushed like feathers.

The entrance hall opened into a grand ballroom, towering ceilings with zealous, religious frescoes painted on every available surface. Solid gold and crystal chandeliers hung low, women threaded through them like supple, hanging fabric. More women congregated around champagne fountains, dipping into them like hummingbirds.

The high rollers sat in the very center of the ballroom—wanting services, but also wanting to be seen and envied. Those conspicuous consumers stretched out on a huge, black, velvet loveseat. Several seated men reclined in their pressed blue suits, their faces entranced and their palms full of cash, booze, breasts, and thighs. Naked women draped all over the men like wilting lilies. They let themselves fall like lotus leaves into the arms of the men and folded themselves into their laps. Each woman had giant doe eyes and the glimmer of a smirk when the men would look away. Many feigned passivity as the men stroked their egos, and occasionally their cocks. One by one, honey bees led the men away from the main room. A siren would take hold of both a man's hands, pull him to his feet, and lead him away with a trail of melodic, maniacal laughter. She would slither away, a man right on her tail, straight to the back rooms, where they'd be concealed in a billowing ocean of royal blue curtains. She would disappear behind the surging waves of fabric, and he would, of course, follow her into the swell, leading with the bow of his ship straight to his own demise, ready to crash into whatever presented itself behind those waves.

My own disaster would be much less dramatic, considering my slender wallet, or so I assumed. I never made it to the black velvet couch; instead, I meekly searched out my woman, calling out to her as I had at the train. But a coral of dark, ringlet-crazy hair obstructed my gaze. This woman looked at me with those huge eyes and pouted her cherry-stained lips—God, those juiced lips—only upstaged by her coffee skin, all flecked in gold like Christmas ribbon. She had an accent that dipped and peaked with aviary tails. Her cadence undulated like the sidewalks and streets. She whispered in my ear that she wanted to undulate on top of me, too. But this wasn't my woman. Dripping with clear diamonds as if shooting stars had shattered all over her, this woman exuded glamour. I could only think to ask her, "Are the waters bluer where you're from?" My wallet in my hand, she took one glossy, manicured finger and peeked inside. She gave me a genuine smile and a kiss on the cheek, and proceeded to strut right past me, diamonds and all.

I didn't see my woman. I didn't even know her name. I'd recognize her distinctive buzzing, her gait from when she'd fled down the stairs of the train station. An assembly of faded Hepplewhite chairs was crowded together at the edge of the room, and I took a seat. It wasn't long before a woman's form poured into my lap. She had a gorgeous complexion, her hair pulled up to the top of her head and her cheekbones jutting out like an emerald mine.

She wrapped her arms around me, buzzing sweet nothings into my ear, and collected every last bit of pollen from my wallet, strapping it to the garter belt around her ankle. I didn't have a say—*or anything to say*—as she pulled me up from the chair, both my hands in hers, and led me into a sheer-curtained room lit all around like a holy altar by candles. She instructed me to lay down amongst the ornate pillows embroidered with silk thread, which were thrown about the floor. She stood before me and I could only stare, mouth agape. One endless leg at a time, she moved over me, the immaculate heart of a prostitute glowing visibly between her covered breasts. She slid her panties down, bending at the hip—her little seduction. With her fingers, she spread herself lewdly, opening like a rose, all pink inside, showing me the place where she would accommodate me into the palace that was her body.

Divinity in its most unexpected form, she towered as an altar herself, ready to be worshiped. The body of a woman, unhidden. She continued to touch herself, practicing her own rituals of self-worship in front of a layman like me. I had no petals to throw at her feet, no precious oils to rub into her skin, no elixirs or riches or anything beyond the last twenties in my wallet to sacrifice to her. She was the altar.

Her hair devastated me, it's glossy, homogeneous perfection all pinned back with silver combs. I could hardly identify its color in such a dimly lit room, distorted as it was by candle flames.

She bent at both knees and lowered herself down to a straddle. I pressed into her. As she rolled over me, her sculpted hair bounced and quivered. Moaning, she ran her hands down her neck, over her arms and breasts. Her hips fell to lusting thighs, those thighs which spoke to me in tongues I often could not discern. She never reached for her hair.

Her fingers caressed all over my shirted chest, but I could only focus on her pulled hair. She wrapped her arms around herself coyly, giving me a cute smile and the flutter of her eyelashes. I surely looked bewildered; she took my face into her hands and asked me if I thought she was beautiful. I nodded. She was; however, with her libidinous movements, strands of her hair untucked themselves from the blinding comb. Entire sections were unpinning themselves and falling down around her face. The strands came down hissing, cursing at me. She looked more and more like Medusa, and I couldn't move—my body turned into stone.

The increasing entropy made me panicky, emotional. I wanted nothing more than for her to tie her hair back up in the perfection it had been, as orderly as the earliest universe. She frowned down at me, at my distracted face. She pulled my hands toward her breasts, using my fingers to expose a pertinent nipple. She licked her lips and gave me a wild smile, which sunk back into a frown when my fingers failed to press into her spilling breast. Her hair continued to cascade, and she commanded me to look at her rather than the ceiling above.

I stared at her face, and it began to pull in points and round in others. The feminine of her face turned feline, and her cat face hissed just like her hair, ready to attack. Her movements became increasingly rapid and frantic. My hands fell from hers and my arms fell back to my sides, sinking into the floor like waterlogged lungs. Her moaning started to sound more and more genuine, to the point where I wondered if this was still just an act. Her fingers found my forearms and she clawed at me, arching like a feline. Those yellow eyes closed, her head tilted back, and I held my breath as her silver comb clacked to the floor. The rest of her hair tumbled down her shoulders, swirled into a black hole—like the universe dying, like I was dying. Her paws gripping me, she opened up like a million flowers on top of me, all coming into season, and her, at once. Breathy and desperate, her body tensed up, and mine too, until I released, and I was the sacrifice. She collapsed on top of me, and I cooled and hardened like obsidian glass after a volcanic disaster.

Unraveling from me, she opened her eyes, and she looked like Juliet's first awakening, flushed and all woman again. Dead or stone, I couldn't move. When our eyes rejoined, she frowned again.

"Did I feel good baby?" she asked me, feigning lust.

An unexpected fury rose from somewhere deep inside of me. "If I am paying you," I muttered, "you should make sure your hair doesn't look like shit."

Confusion painted her face; she stood up, hands in her hair and honey dripping down her legs. She came to me; pulled me into her. "Did you not enjoy yourself, baby?" she crooned into my ear, probably still hoping for a tip.

I shoved her away with a grimace. "Your fucking hair is everywhere; it's a mess."

Her chest sank as her hand sprung up against it, to protect her heart from my words. I was so angry. *Why was I so angry?*

"Without all of the polishing, you look just like all those other whores."

Her heart cracked open like the bulb of a thermometer. Glass shards ripped toward me, and poisonous mercury dripped from a hole in her chest. Fur formed on her face again as it pulled into that animal way. I had turned her rabid. Her hands whipped out around her as she grabbed every candle she could reach and hurled them all at me. Searing hot wax covered my forearms and burned into my skin. I screamed at her, this *bitch*. I reached for her neck, but she dodged my hand. I balled that same hand into a fist and went after her. Before I could land a single punch, the bitch kicked me right between my legs and I went down. She pounded me with pillows, her fists, and whatever else she could reach. Down feathers now adhered themselves to the wax on my forearms. She slashed at my face with her cat claws.

Taking a step back, she looked me up and down—me, tarred and feathered, bloody—examining her work. She stood there and her smirk turned into laughter—that maniacal laughter. Her stilettos waded through the sea of glass she had crushed on the ground as she left the curtained room. She stopped and turned back to me, still smirking. Her hand to her lips, she blew me a kiss, and it was a kiss that materialized in green smoke and floated innocently toward me, slapping me on the cheek with a sizzle and the smell of burning flesh. She turned and strutted out of the room like…like there wasn't blood and blisters running down my forearms, like this beautiful room hadn't been destroyed. The vile, screaming kiss tunneled through my flesh, digging into my veins where it surged its poisonous color through my body. The kiss coursed through me, sinister and nauseating. Its trail still burned through the air; my pulse quickened and my own traitorous body helped pump her sex magic through the entirety of my fallible body.

I summoned up all of the strength that I could and stood, unsteady and swaying like a 5 a.m. drunk. Furious, incited, I screamed for someone in charge. Many beaded curtains jingled as worker bees and patrons alike peeked their heads through to see what the hell I was yelling about. I heard a woman's reassuring voice drift down the aisle, closer and closer to the alcove in which I stood screaming—where I was lividly ripping off feathers, and my own skin in the process.

The voice came closer and it lulled me into a sense of calm, my nerves becoming more manageable. My body tingled in pleasure instead of searing pain. More beads rattled as she popped each nosey onlooker back into their room and into their own business. I held my breath in anticipation as she approached my room. I was almost gleeful to see the body from which this heavenly voice emanated. A pair of pointy, black, patent leather boots stepped into view under the cheap, orange, beaded curtain that had concealed me.

Lilith parted the curtains and walked inside. Smirking, she crooned, "Still coming to repent for your sins, I see. You didn't enjoy playtime with Virgo? What did you do to deserve her viridescent curse?" And the relief that had poured into me at the sound of that angelic voice immediately crashed into sickness, and my injuries seemed to burn more intensely now. My stomach rotted in anxiety and my pulse pounded.

FOUR

Lilith wore her full armor: platform heels, skintight dress, whip in hand. I stood bleeding and burning, melting before her smirking visage. With a courage I'd never had as a teenager, I spun away from the Hive Queen and ran. I tore through the beaded curtain, and it jangled violently right back at me, each bead infuriated and cursing me straight to Hell. I ran desperately through the brothel, the sound of Virgo's deviled laughter tailing me as if I were prey. I pushed past beautiful, rich women in a frenzy, each one adding their own perturbation to the chorus that hunted me. The great, ancient oak doors opened and spit me out, slamming behind me with a heavy final thud. A cold fall of rain soothed my wretched skin. Virgo's curse crawled through my veins, shifting me through moments of fever in which my vision hazed and everything around me became a terrible mirage.

I ran down broken streets, their potholes overflowing with black water and street lights reflecting from puddles like rippling, watching eyes. I rounded the corner at Hubbard and continued my sprint along an abandoned row of factories. My legs and lungs ached, but horror and adrenaline forced my legs to continue their forward lurch. I hit Cane Avenue, only a few blocks away from sanctuary. Turning the corner, I found myself illuminated in the safe pink glow of a familiar neon sign.

I stumbled into the Little Midnight Diner—panting, soaked with rain, forearms still tender from wax—dropping feathers behind me that found freedom in the wind. The waitress, Maria, looked concerned. Her face held soft smile lines that I could see even when she frowned. Her hair was pulled back into a sparkly plastic clip and fell down to her shoulders. A modest gold pendant strung around her slight neck glistened under the fluorescent lights. Her body, full and pregnant, swelled underneath a white apron.

She dropped her tray of dirty dishes next to the bus pan and rushed over to me. Taking my hands, empathy seeped from her eyes into the sullen parts of my face. Her eyelids were smeared with shimmery purple eyeshadow and a pretty pink blush colored her cheeks. Lacquered eyelashes fluttered as she blinked. She reached her warm palms up to my cold, damp cheeks. Even her smile lines were frowning now.

"What the hell happened to you?" she asked bluntly.

I shrugged. Maria shifted her doubtful eyes to my arms, and her fuchsia cheeks began to soften into butterfly wings. Her eyes pulled into the corners of the forming chitin and her face began to flap gently. The butterfly-faced woman let her hands fall from my face down to my own hands once again. She turned away from me, pulling me to follow, just as Virgo had done not even an hour before. Letting a woman lead means to risk either paradise or perdition. I could still see her forewings as she flew us down a windowed line of vinyl-seated booths, right past the cobwebs and the mouse traps and the peeling paint.

Maria pushed me into the last booth, and I sat facing the wall like I always did. She flew away in her pale pink dress and sensible shoes. I stared at the wall. I never could see what she was doing from my coveted seat, but she was always doing something good. This night, she pulled a jacket out of the lost and found. She warmed a towel under the hot lamp and dampened another in the sink. She poured up a decaf coffee with a dollop of whipped cream. She told her husband in the back kitchen to whip up some eggs and toast. He massaged butter into the hot griddle, getting ready to cook something to soothe my broken soul.

The butterfly-faced woman flew back with the jacket, the two towels, the coffee with whipped cream, and the plate of rich breakfast food. She sat next to me, folding one leg under her, with the cocoon of her belly forcing space between us. She took the damp towel and started working on my burned forearms, peeling off the remaining wax and feathers, and occasionally my skin, too. She wiped the blood from my scared face. Her amethyst heart glowed soft and purple from beneath her collar-covered breasts as she worked. Some of the feathers were too painful to pull away. Their needles stuck to my arms as if they were growing out of my skin.

"Take off this shirt."

And I did, glancing around the Little Midnight Diner at the few other diners, making sure they were busy with their newspapers or passed out drunk. Maria patted my skin dry with the warm towel, then folded it up and laid it on the back of my neck. She gave me the jacket from the lost-and-found—a navy Harrington—and I pulled it tenderly over my arms, zipping it over my bare chest. I ate the food; I drank the coffee. Warm and full, I fell asleep at the booth. I had gone through this ritual many times.

Maria was the best that this world had to offer. Years ago, I had stumbled into the diner drunk, my knuckles still sore from punching brick walls in my intoxicated fury. I was broke, unemployed, and homeless, as I'd been ever since the night Eva had disappeared. I remember that night: Maria fed me, listened to my furious monologue about my world turning against me, and quieted my infantile wailing. Ever since that night, she had provided me this sanctuary, which is one that I'm sure she has provided to many: warmth, a meal, a few hours of quiet rest. She fluttered around, attending to her customers while always keeping a watchful eye on me. She, my butterfly angel sent down from Heaven. An angel of simple comforts, a virginal mother who didn't have to fuck my father to feel maternal toward me.

Black night still filled the diner windows when I woke up. The table had been cleared, and my shirt sat dry and folded on the clean linoleum. I stuffed it into the pocket of my new, hand-me-down jacket and started toward the door. Maria perched at the counter. She pulled a cup of coffee to her lips, its rim stained and shimmering pink from her lipstick. Her faintly creased eyes perused a newspaper from under her fluttering eyelashes. She turned to me and gave me that warm Maria smile. Patting the vanilla vinyl seat beside her, she motioned for me to join her.

Reluctantly, I sat. I wasn't much of a conversationalist when I wasn't fall-down drunk. She pulled my hand into hers, and her eyes flapped at me gently, the narrows of her winged face softening.

"What happened to you, Cas?" Concern rang in the timber of her voice, yet her face remained ethereal.

My own face, however, went deeply red. "I was at home," I lied, "and I…I fell near my bedside table. I had some candles burning…. I must have grabbed a pillow or something to catch my fall…and I…"

I quieted myself as Maria smirked at my bullshit story. The shimmering violet of her eyes traced the cat scratches down my neck. She grabbed a hand mirror from the pocket of her apron and dared me to look at my own image.

Purple bruising and claw marks that were thin as veins graphed my face. They looked inconspicuous compared to the noxious set of green lips embossed on my right cheek. My stomach twisted and my face radiated the heat of shame. Maria smirked and licked the corner of a napkin, rubbing it against the kiss firmly. To my surprise, and my immense relief, the napkin came back green; Maria had wiped that sinister kiss right off my face. Did that mean the curse was broken? Had I outrun the curse just as John had so many years earlier?

"Emerald, huh? Not a lot of women could pull that off. So, what? Did your girlfriend catch you cheating or something?" Maria asked.

I shook my head. How could I tell this woman, who resided on a much higher ethereal plane than I ever would, that I had been branded by some bitch in a brothel? The glow of Maria's unborn baby sparkled off her skin; this was an image of perfection, purity, holiness, and all that was decent, how could I reveal myself as a deviant?

She leaned in with a smile. "It's okay," she whispered. "I don't want to pry. She really did a number on you, though!" Her sentence ended in a giggle.

I looked down at my forearms. "I think she might have cursed me." I smirked, feigning a joke. But Maria raised a thick eyebrow at me.

"…cursed?"

Again, I blushed. I quickly attempted to redact the imbecile words that had spilled from my mouth. "I just mean, you know…not really cursed, just…."

Again, she raised an eyebrow and tilted her head, the wings of her face beginning to animate once more. She glanced over the feathers peeking out from the sleeves of the jacket and then to the green-smudged napkin.

With one long finger—the nail painted blue and iridescent—she beckoned me close and lowered her voice to a murmur.

"Cas, there are forces on this earth that we maybe can't see, but that doesn't mean they aren't working around us."

Her hand rested on mine now.

I stuttered.

"I… I…."

Maria put her finger to my lips. She looked around at the booths, mostly empty at this hour, and turned a suspicious eye toward her husband. "If you think this girl has powers, well, that's not something you want to play around with, believe me. When you work these kinds of hours, hours where not a lot of people are around, you start to notice things."

I broke her gaze as my stomach began to sink. Eva had made it impossible for me to ignore how the reality of earth pulsed with both magic and the Divine. People don't notice it because they are too enthralled in their own lives, running from goal to goal until they eventually run into their graves. The Divine doesn't spend its time on the gleaming avenues of affluent neighborhoods, and it doesn't care about the lavish towers of wealth that men build to honor it. Simple creatures know how to worship the Divine under high branches that arc like vaulted ceilings. Fish document Genesis in mosaics of freshwater pebbles on river floors. The stumps of ancient, dead trees grasp the earth, down to the rock, and become holy sepulchers in which old things become new again, and life is fostered in this wooden crib.

You find the Divine at your rock bottom, in the shittiest of places. The reflection blinking back up at you from the bottom of your fourth whiskey sour, in some hole in the wall place—that is Divinity. The Queen of Hearts, exposing her breasts from your palm, flattened on the pavement in some back-alley poker game—she is the Divine.

A losing lottery ticket that refuses to change your life, that's divine intervention. Black mold seeps from underneath the sink of my upstairs neighbor, darkening my ceiling, and this will certainly be the divine master of my death.

The Divine comes to us when there is no good, wholesome, earthly thing left to be seen. When our lives fall apart, when purpose alludes us, there it is, Divinity, winking at us from all of the wrong places, eager to bring us to the brink of our own madness;

and humankind in our weakness cannot help but to over-indulge in the sanctity of divine things. A whore house is just the kind of place that would be crawling with divine creatures.

I looked up at Maria and nodded, as I had been cursed. Again, she dropped her voice, eyeing her husband as she spoke.

"Look, I don't talk about this much because my husband thinks it's all devil worship."

I looked over at her husband: a thick gold cross swayed from his neck over the griddle as he worked, imbuing the food with contrived holiness as he worked.

Maria caught my eye and continued, "I know a lady, a lady that might be able to help. You see this?" She patted her belly with both hands. "This is all her!" I raised an eyebrow and Maria laughed. "I mean, of course, we had a little something to do with it, too."

She nodded toward her husband diligently cleaning the grill in preparation for the imminent 4 a.m. rush.

"We tried for so long to have a baby, and it just never took. The doctors said we were too old, and there wasn't anything they could really do for us. One day, I was taking out the garbage, and there was this homeless lady chowing down on some of the stale bread we'd thrown in the garbage."

The bells at the door of the diner chimed, and a man fought with his umbrella as he stepped inside and took a seat at the counter. Maria stood and went behind the counter, retrieving a gleaming white coffee cup from underneath it. She held one finger up at me, instructing me to hold on as she went over to serve the man. She smiled at him warmly, pouring him a hot, black cup of coffee and sliding a menu in front of him. I watched the man pick out a couple of flavored creamers as Maria made her way back to my end of the diner. Leaning over with her elbows on the counter, she again dropped her voice.

"Anyway, so there was that homeless lady eating out of the garbage, and I invited her to come inside. She was real…

eccentric—*real* eccentric. My husband was shooting me looks the whole time, like 'Why did you let this crazy lady in here?', but you know he's not really gonna say anything about it because it's really me who makes the rules." She winked. "So, she had on a bathrobe and pointy shoes, and long white hair, too—an older woman—and, well, she looked like a witch!" Laughter punctuated her sentence. "So, anyway, I fed her, and she was kind of staring at me the whole time, and I'm thinking, I don't know, maybe the woman isn't right."

The man held up a finger, and Maria fluttered right over to him, taking his order—always with a smile—and refilling the cup of coffee he'd already emptied. She wrote his order on a notepad and passed the sheet back to her husband, blowing him a little kiss. A sweet kiss, not an accursed one.

She fluttered back to me, perching once again on the counter, and settled back into her thoughts, continuing her story, "So, this lady, well, so she wasn't really saying her 'please and thank yous'; she wasn't really saying anything at all, which was okay, because I figured she must be living a hard life out there, you know? But then, suddenly, I'm clearing her plate, and she kind of, lands her hand on my belly. This was months ago, you know, and I was like, 'Okay?' and she says, 'You've been trying for a long time, haven't you?' I didn't even register that she was talking about a baby at first! I was just like, looking at her like, *huh?* But that's all she said, so I went back to the kitchen to put the plates in the sink, and then she was gone. I forgot all about it."

A few more customers filed in, along with a busboy ready for his shift. Slick rain raced down from umbrellas and trench coats to come to rest on the glistening floor. Maria said 'hello' to everyone, fluttering away with her coffee cups and that pot of hot, fragrant coffee in her hands, a bundle of menus under her arm. After making her rounds, she stood right next to me again.

She continued, "So, I forget about her, right? I go home around, I don't know, 9 a.m., and I get some sleep. I come back to the diner that night, and she's sitting on that old bench out front. I'm thinking she's just hungry again, but no, she doesn't want to come inside, she wants to talk. So, I sat down, too, and she started asking me about if I'd ever wanted to have kids. So, I started telling her about how I very much wanted to have kids, but that it never happened for us."

Behind me, I could hear the slap of a mop gobbling up all the water that had accumulated by the door.

"So, I tell her all of this, and she digs around in her bathrobe and pulls out one of those honey bottles that are shaped like a bear. She stirred a bunch of little flowers into it, and it looked pretty, kind of like that New Age stuff. But then she tells me to eat the stuff, take a big tablespoon every day, and then an extra tablespoon to rub all over my belly. Then she said I should cut up a persimmon, a *persimmon*, into quarters, put it under my bed on the first night that I take the honey, and only throw it out when the honey is up. And I'm just smiling and nodding, thinking, 'Wow, this woman really isn't right, huh?' So, I take the stuff and thank her, and she leaves. Well, that morning when I got home, I got to thinking like, how did she know that I had been trying? I'm not exactly a young woman anymore, and I know my husband would never bring it up with anyone, let alone some crazy woman. So, I don't know. I decided, *hey, it couldn't hurt to try*, not really expecting it to do anything. I go to the market, buy a persimmon, cut it up, and put it under my bed, praying the ants won't get to it. I eat the honey, I rub up my belly with it, and I wrap myself in some cloth so it won't get all over my bed. My husband never even noticed! Two weeks after I finished the bottle, I missed my time…. We'd given up, honestly. It's a miracle, but it was that woman! She moved whatever energy was blocking the baby, I think, and I bet you she will know what to do about your girlfriend, too!" Maria ended her story with a smile and fluttered off to tend her diner.

I knew exactly who Maria was talking about. As a kid, I saw

that woman talking to herself around the city, screaming at people who weren't there and wailing from treetops. I was always terrified of her. As we got older, me and my friends would alternate between the brothel and the alley that the old woman lived in. We'd listen to her mumble to herself as she rattled through her hordes of junk and we'd laugh at this insane homeless woman. Once, we arrived at the mouth of the alley and it was silent; she wasn't home. We dared each other to venture inside, egging each other on until, finally, someone did dare. He crept inside, all of us acting cool while our insides bundled up in anxiety. The boy walked up to a pile of milk crates and kicked them over. They came crashing down, all their contents chiming with the sounds of broken glass. But as the crates clattered to the ground, we suddenly heard the lashing bark of vicious dogs. Big, black rottweilers had seemingly sprung up from Hell and pounded through the alley, straight for us. We all turned on our heels, sprinting away as fast as we could, with the boy who kicked the crates over following quite a length behind. We were able to clamber over a chain link fence, the massive dogs on hind legs behind us, foaming at the mouth. That was our last visit to the alley.

Maria didn't know where to find the woman, but I assured her that I did. Her alley, a narrow dead-end, divided Marmora and St. Clair. *Eva had lived on Marmora.* I thanked Maria for her kindness, her hospitality, and her warmth. She hugged me and asked me to stop by when I wasn't in a crisis for once. Crisis, my status quo.

FIVE

Deep in the heart of the abandoned industrial sector lived the homeless sorceress. Through the pouring rain, a great plume of violet smoke rose from behind one of the old factories, its wet, broken windows glistening like jagged pools of starlight. I tore behind it, into the mouth of a claustrophobic, dead-end of an alley, and there she was—the high priestess of our world—standing behind an enormous fire which had been lit inside an aluminum garbage can and which raged on despite the pouring rain.

She stood in a tattered gray bathrobe, splattered in mud and paint, and her long, frazzled white hair hung lewdly against her shoulders. The rain—she either didn't notice or didn't care—poured down upon her like a baptism. She didn't acknowledge me. Her eyes were closed, and she muttered to herself, or to the fire, or to someone I couldn't see.

The woman had tarps hung from each wall—makeshift tents keeping all of her worldly possessions dry. She'd strung up two tarps into a canopy to conceal her personal living quarters. Bundles and bundles of plant matter, tied together with what appeared to be cassette tape, were stacked up against one of the walls. Like a raven's nest full of stolen shiny objects, her own accumulation of random metal things could be seen. Broken watches, an assortment of tarnished chains, picture frames, goblets, and teaspoons. On one of the walls, she had hung tapestries; pieces of fabric and rope tied into makeshift patterns. Her shopping cart overflowed with the treasures she had picked up from her travels; bundles of rope, broken pieces of wood, unmatched couch cushions, well-used watercolor sets, and a ton of yellowed books on any given topic.

I stepped closer to the fire, as the warmth of the diner had long subsided. I put my hands up to the flames, and as if sensing my energy coming through them, she opened her eyes and gave me a good up-and-down. She said nothing.

I cleared my throat and willed my vocal cords to assert themselves.

"Uh, yeah. I was sent to you by…uh, by a friend. I-I need your help." She fumbled around her alley—looking for something, ignoring my words.

"My friend," I continued, "she, uh, she works at the diner. She and her husband own it, actually. She said you helped them…."

The sorceress found what she was looking for, and I watched her throw a handful of leaves into the fire, turning the flames the same amethyst as Maria's shimmery eyeshadow, the same amethyst as her heart.

I felt annoyed by her disregard, but the raw, singed, cursed skin on my forearms served as a reminder of the consequences of my temper.

"Well, so, I think I've been cursed," I said casually. "And while I don't know the extent of this curse, I figure it can't be good." I smiled; she did not.

Finally, she stopped fooling around in her piles of junk, and she looked at me.

"A curse?" she asked the wall next to her.

She hobbled over to an old, gaudy armchair, another plastic tarp hanging above it. The small woman sank right into the deep, midnight fabric. It looked like she had repaired the chair with snakes of black electrical tape, which worked their way all along its structure. I could barely see her over the fire. She took one long, knobby finger and beckoned me to her.

"Pull up a milk crate and sit with me, boy."

Boy? I was no boy; I was a man. My brow furrowed in annoyance, but again, my pride had done enough damage for the night. I did as I was told.

"Tell me about this curse." she said.

My face reddened. I decided to take a more mild path around the truth. "Well, I got into a fight with this girl, and I said some things I shouldn't have, and I really pissed her off. She attacked me and then blew me a kiss from across the room. But I could actually see it—this pair of green lips floated at me through the air! The lips hit my cheek, and when they hit, it felt like…a sear, and I felt...something, all through my body."

I'd been wide-eyed as I'd explained these limited details. The sorceress smirked at me just like Maria had.

"A kiss that floats through the air, huh? That sounds like sex magic to me, dear."

The red in my face deepened and my forearms itched. "I don't know what kind of magic it is, I just want it gone," I sputtered out, embarrassed. She knew exactly where I had been.

Still smirking, she said, "Well, I can't help you, dear, if I don't know the complete and accurate account of the curse."

I scowled at her through the flames. She enjoyed my burning shame and wanted me to recount my deviancy aloud. With a deep breath, I began. I told her how I'd visited the Theater, how Virgo had sought me out, how her sex was good, but her hair a mess. I explained how I'd insulted her, how I'd lunged at her in anger. Though my pride ached, I even admitted how Virgo had fought back, her face pulled into a feline cast. How she'd overcome me, and left me tarred, feathered, and bloody, with a sickening green kiss on my cheek.

The smirk of the sorceress had faded, and her features held still, severe.

"The women in the Theater are goddesses," she said, "women capable of immense power. Whether they practice for good or for evil, they, like me, are all high priestesses of the Divine. We often choose to spend our earthly reign among the truest and trying of human conditions."

The sorceress reclined back into her chair and closed her eyes.

"Virgo is the Honey Goddess. She is the sweet goddess of the soft heart. She values gentleness and tender care. Virgo allowed you to pray at her altar, and you responded with violence."

"I was angry!" I pleaded.

"Your anger is not an excuse for your actions. Many men have realized their inferiority in the presence of a goddess, a supreme being that maybe they don't immediately recognize, who they cannot identify with. And this has meant the downfall for a great many of these men."

The sorceress' dark, lined eyes bored into me.

"How do I fix this?" I asked.

"I know what you must do, but I won't tell you without an offering," she said with a chuckle.

I frowned again. "An offering?"

Almost incredulously, she repeated, "An offering, yes, an offering, of course, an offering! I am of the Divine, and I want to see some devotion!" She smiled a toothy smile, exposing many black gaps. I had nothing to give and no idea what she would want.

I turned out my jean pockets and pulled out a stick of gum, tacky from sitting in my soaking wet pocket, as well as my empty wallet, a Queen of Hearts card that had won me $500 once, and Eva's broken necklace. The sorceress looked into my hands, skepticism all over her face.

"This is all you have?"

I shrugged my shoulders. Virgo had taken all of the money, and dignity, I'd had.

The sorceress plucked the Queen of Hearts from my hand. "Well, I'll take this, of course."

Of course, she could recognize the degenerate's Divine. She fingered the necklace next, an eyebrow raised in surprise.

"Why are you carrying this?"

I shrugged my shoulders. I had been on my way to pawn it when I'd seen my woman at the train. The chain alone was 24-karat gold, and who knew what the stones were worth? I had kept it for so long, but Eva wasn't coming back.

"I don't know. It's just some of my ex's costume jewelry," I lied.

She took it from my hands and threaded it upon a tree branch. She faced the fire.

"I really don't want to let that go, though. We broke up, you know; it's a memory…."

Ignoring my lies, she thrust the branch into the fire, the valuable necklace swinging wildly among the flames.

"What are you doing!?" I cried, my hands in my hair at the sight of my next meal ticket being consumed in flames.

The fire responded with violent height, glowing pale and pink—vicious despite its soft parade of color—before settling into a gentle swell, like a cotton candy sunset. The old lady pulled the branch back. The intact and unblemished gold chain swung from the black, ashen wood.

Thank God.

The sorceress looked at me. "How did you get Eva's necklace?"

My brows furrowed, confused. "How the fuck do you know her name is Eva?"

"It is Eva's necklace," she responded, ignoring my question.

Had Eva come to see this lunatic before disappearing?

The old woman took the necklace off the branch and pocketed it next to the Queen of Hearts.

"I'm not giving you that necklace." I said firmly.

"It is not your necklace to give. If you don't want my advice, I will give you back the Queen of Hearts; however, this necklace must be returned to Eva."

A hot temper began to pool in my veins again.

"No one knows where Eva is; she's gone! If she's not dead she's forgotten all about it."

The woman sat back in her armchair and said nothing.

"Give me the fucking necklace!" I barked. The woman sat in silence. I stepped closer to her, unsure of exactly what I was going to do. Before I could figure it out, I heard growling from the deepest black of the alley. Two dogs slithered toward me, closing the gap between me and the sorceress. The flames in the garbage can licked cobalt blue.

I practically flew back to the mouth of the alley. "Please!" I said, though I wasn't sure what I was pleading for.

"Well, I am willing to accept this offering because you have a lesson to learn, and it would do us all some good if you learned it," she said simply.

"Fine," I said, defeated, "what do I have to do?"

Again, she stood and approached the fire, which had settled to a quite mundane orange. "A woman must be prayed to like an altar, and in order to break this curse, you must pray to the altar of Virgo."

Jesus. I had to shut my eyes to stop them from rolling. "All right, so where is it?" I asked bluntly, with a frown. *What a dumb thing to do; pray to a hooker.*

The sorceress laughed.

"You come to me, cursed by the immaculate Virgo, and you ask, where is her altar? Where do I pray?" She continued to giggle.

Fuck this obnoxious woman.

"To pray to the altar of Virgo is to perform her ritual worship."

I exhaled hard. What the fuck did that mean?

Another chuckle. "Be thankful, dear, that the Honey Goddess's ritual is among the more tepid. Now, had you been cursed by Diana, that would have been bloody." Her laugh turned sinister.

I ran my hands over my face. What the hell had I gotten myself into?

"How do I perform her ritual?" I asked. God, my forearms really burned now.

"The ritual must be performed with a full heart and beauty." The sorceress rummaged around in one of her carts as she spoke. "You care for her with sweetness, you savor her like a nectar, and you perform the ritual cleanse with this sacred elixir."

She pulled out an orange plastic bottle that read, *Relaxing Milk & Honey Body Wash*. An aggressive red sticker pasted on the front yelled, *$.99!*

Sitting back in her throne, the homeless sorceress continued, "You need forbidden fruit for the offering, braid lavender and honeysuckle into her hair, and bee balm for the feet."

I stuck out three fingers—*lavender, honeysuckle, bee balm*—ticking each flower off on a new digit.

She continued, "If she is happy with your worship, if she is lulled to a careless calm, she will allow you to pray at her altar. Should you appease her, she will cut the curse from you like a dead limb. But if you don't, well…."

Eyeing the feathers that poked out from under my sleeves, she put the bottle of body wash in my hands. I stared at this dollar bin find, wondering why I was taking advice from a deranged woman.

It was late—or very early, depending on how your circadian rhythm functioned. The rain clouds blew over with gusto, as if terrified of the rising sun. My legs felt leaden, every muscle drained. I walked through the streets feeling unsure of what works the curse intended within me, avoiding alleyways as they pulsed and seethed with unknown monsters. Hot steam rose from between buildings, and every now and then, I would peer down and see a gleam of silver scales, or hear the tail end of a ferocious roar. My shitty apartment building looked like the Garden of Eden compared to the night I'd had. The old stoop glittered with broken glass; maybe all the stars had fallen right out of the sky and shattered just to remind me that there was no serenity in the cosmos.

SIX

I lived in a shitty building that my uncle had tried to convert into a motel decades ago. It's rumored among the family that he wanted to compete with the Theater, wanted to create his own hive, but he also wanted a substantial cut of the honey—and the hunnies, too. Worker bees don't easily bide to fumbling bears pawing for honeycomb and a palm-full of ass. The next time the family saw him, he had mangled and swollen hands; he explained only that he'd gotten caught reaching into the cookie jar. After that, he cycled through month-to-month tenants like seasons until I moved in and became his sole long-term resident, even though I barely paid the rent. The building was a crimson-bricked two-flat, stuffed with crumbling drywall and toxic, bubble-gum insulation. A length of neon lighting molded into a giant heart hung against the east-facing facade, screaming:

LOVER'S MOTEL
COLOR TV
AIR CONDITIONING
TELEPHONES

I couldn't ever remember a time when this place hadn't been a shithole—dated, and completely neglected. The limestone stoop spilled out onto a vibrant canvas of sidewalk graffiti. A plastic green awning reached over a second-floor balcony that lined the side of the building. Artificial grass covered the floor, this being my uncle's attempt at increasing property value with some green space. Historically, it was this balcony where every occupant in the place had smoked, thrown out their trash, and fought with their red-fisted boyfriends.

My second-floor apartment was one large room which overlooked the main street, and I passed a lot of my time watching people living out their lives underneath where I wasted mine. The seasons changed, and people shifted through them, transfixed in their routines and clinging to the familiarity of what they knew. There was the man who came to visit *his* woman, who lived across the street from me. Every Friday, he came dressed to the nines: suit, tie, draper hat, polished scarps, and always with an arm-full of long-stemmed gladiolus. How that woman's face would glow at the sight of her lover! All the way from across the street, I could see how her cheeks still flushed a deep rouge, even though the entire routine was written into her like thin maps of veining. The woman would take the flowers into her arms, and then the man would take her into his; it was a beautiful, time-honored ritual that I hated to miss.

The apartment above theirs belonged to a young girl and her giant black dog. The dog's coat gleamed and feathered out all along his legs, tail, and belly. Their building sat next to a stretch of overgrown, abandoned lots, and the dog would prance through the tall, unkempt grasses, chewing at a few stalks, his nose following flames of monarch butterflies as he panted with excitement and absolute joy. Rabbits populated the field, and the dog would leap after them until they snuggled through a gap in the fence that was much too small for a big, black dog. Still, he would get right up to that fence, beaming at the rabbit and itching to get closer, though his size would never let him pass through the slim opening. The girl would call out to him, *Jack!* He'd turn his attention back to his girl, then moseying on over, he'd nuzzle his sweet, black face against her thigh, her hand stroking his soft ears.

They'd lived across from me for years, and though the girl stayed young, with time, the dog's black coat began to gray, like he had dipped his muzzle into a drift of snow. Still, they kept up their ritual despite the passage of years, and despite the inevitability of a fate that was coming for them faster than either of them could imagine. One morning, I looked out my window and watched Jack chase that same rabbit, as he had done so many times. The rabbit ran through the gap in the fence and—I couldn't believe it—the dog passed his big, black body right through that gap and kept after the rabbit. The bunny got away, into some burrow hole somewhere, but the dog gamboled through the field as best as his arthritic joints would allow, all his joy and jubilation evident in his happy face and wagging tail. The girl stood in her open doorway, wide-eyed and cheering. A kitty with an orange creamsicle coat padded out the door, rubbing against the girl's legs before curling around the legs of the dog who had returned to the side of his beloved companion. The girl looked on with placid eyes, through the dandelion stalks and thick reams of milkweed which extended across the field. She took a bite out of a peach, the juices running down her hand and forearm. She licked at the little streams—savoring every bit of that peach. She wanted to keep tasting and tasting because it was just so sweet.

Later that evening, the sun sat low in the sky and the world looked milky, all blue and yellow. The girl walked down the street with a leash in hand, but no dog. Even from my second-floor window, I could see her face contorted with tears, her hands clinging to her heart as if to keep the broken pieces from falling out of her chest.

The girl stood with her hands laced through the gaping fence. Bushes full of white and purple heaven flowers bloomed against the rusted chain link. The other side grew free and wild, plush and green like a budding forest. The girl took up a ritual of throwing dead flowers through the gap, and as they decayed, the garden would flourish, making dead things beautiful again. Of course, the lot owner would come out on occasion and mow the fields, trying to keep them tame and presentable to avoid city fines. But the fields would always grow back, despite his best efforts, even more wild than before.

So, I sat at this window and watched the lives of others go by, always sure that people from the street could see me, too. In the evenings, I'd turn into a shadow moving through the dimly lit background of my yellow-flowered kitchen, and I'd pretend I was a puppet and put on elaborate shows for the passersby. I would perform impassioned air guitar solos or do cartwheel after cartwheel—more often than not landing hard and raw on my knees. I hoped someone would catch a glimpse of my absurdity, and maybe I would make it into the next day's watercooler chit-chat.

I practically crawled up the steps to my apartment, my legs like lead, arms aching in dull pain. Fumbling with my keys, I finally got my door open and headed straight for my bed. I sat at the edge and slid off my new jacket, careful not to rub the polyester fabric on my tender skin. The pit of my stomach lurched as I examined my forearms. The feathers that the butterfly woman had so carefully peeled away had returned...*and multiplied*! Each quill sprouted from a calamus that was tucked deeply into my flesh. The feathers had snuck far up my forearms, past my shoulders, and down my back. Even my belly sprouted soft white down. Stumbling into the bathroom, I examined myself. Colored like a Sebright chicken, tawny feathers covered my back, and these were much denser than the white feathers all over my front. I stared at myself in the mirror, now unphased by my scarred face and neck, or by the colorless embossing of lips on my cheek. Feathers grew all over my human body.

Several years before, a local man had gone missing. He had left home late in the night, assuring his wife that he would be back soon, insisting that he absolutely could not live without milk for his early-morning coffee, or another pack of cigarettes…whatever excuses men tell their wives to go spend a few hours with another woman. He never came back home and was never heard from again. The only clue investigators had to go on was a pile of his clothes found abandoned at the park. His wife called the hospitals, jails, and bars; no one had seen him. The wife assumed he had run off with some whore, but filed a missing person's report on the insistence of their grown daughter, who could only see decency in her father.

Days later, investigators recovered the man's smart, eggshell button-down, a pair of brown trousers, a leather belt, and sneakers laid out on a park walk. His shirt tucked perfectly into his pant line, and socks still stuffed into the shoes. If they hadn't known any better, the police might have thought the man had evaporated right out of his clothes. The man's wallet—empty of all cash and credit cards, but still housing his ID and several local rewards cards—peeked out from a trouser pocket. Down feathers fluttered over the outfit like snow. Nearby, a chicken lay dead and headless, with deep, red blood pooling from the wound like polished circles of garnet.

Rumors of black magic circulated around town for quite some time. Church attendance increased, and makeshift crosses went up in every yard—made of tied brooms and mops, tree branches, or whatever people had lying around. Any random ritual would surely do the trick. But the man's wife gave him no chance for sympathy. She told anyone who would listen that her dog of a man had faked his own death to escape his commitment to

Men turning into bird

her and the crushing predictability of family life. He'd alleviated himself from the obligation of one more boring family dinner, another weekend spent mowing the lawn and flipping through the channels.

But I remembered how I had forgone my nightly walks to the Theater when the man went missing. I'd been afraid of an unknown evil, afraid of whatever had happened to him. I had seen him at the Theater the night before he went missing. I remembered how he cursed the very heavens themselves as he stomped out the front door, scalded and covered in feathers. Just like I had been.

I couldn't look at myself anymore. Leaving the bathroom, I closed the door behind me to avoid catching sight of my feathered body. I put the milk and honey body wash on the warped top of my wooden kitchen table.

Women use their beauty as a weapon; they lure us in, and take advantage of our good nature. Virgo was no forbidden fruit; she was no prize. Now, she wanted to emasculate me with this curse. Anger fueled demons inside me, the origins of which I didn't understand. *If I killed her*, I thought, *maybe the curse would be broken*. If she left this earth, how could her powers keep their hold over me as I continued to walk it? She's a streetwalker, a brothel bee. Who would mourn the death of this unclean woman? Who would report her missing? Who would care even if her absence was noticed?

I took a seat at the table. The chair wobbled on the uneven hardwood. My face was unsure whether it should deepen the furrows in my brow or darken the circles under my eyes. I looked through the apartment at the dusty light filtering in from my windows. A glass of stale water rested on my bedside table from days before. The sun shot through it, throwing rainbows all over the old, orange carpet. I stood and rummaged through the drawers of my wardrobe until I found a pocket knife. I put it out on the table but then I slipped it into my jeans pocket, altogether unsure of what I was planning.

The sun came into the morning too bright, and too yellow. The day too clear, with too blue a sky, too generic and perfect. I flopped onto my mattress, which was covered in old checkered sheets. Floral print cases loosely covered my pillows. Feminine, but I liked them, and I never had any guests anyway. No one had to know that I enjoyed the few hours of sleep I could manage with my head resting on seas of violets and daisies.

The pillowcases had been Eva's. I'd hated them when they were hers, but somehow, they'd ended up in the box of her things that I'd taken after she left. Going through her house was an insurmountable task. Eva was a curator of common things and her home was a junk museum. Things that didn't matter to sensible people mattered exceptionally to her. She wanted her objects to have eternal life; in fact, that responsibility to care for all of her things kept her tethered to her house for so long. Nothing meant more to her—nothing. She left pages and pages of notes describing the importance of every item in her house. She made it explicitly clear that she wanted everything treasured, nothing thrown away. For me, it was hell.

Instead of dealing with it, I asked her closest friends and family to go through her home and choose objects of hers to keep. For many years, Eva had preferred to isolate herself, and had chosen the company of her things over everyone else. Many of her friends had given up, and I'd never seen most of the faces that showed up to her home before. A number of strangers let themselves in, too, looking to find valuables among the madness that made up Eva's home. They left her home picked through, but largely intact and full, almost as she had left it.

I moved through the house alone, like we had done so many times before. I wasn't looking for treasure; I wanted the routine. With my eyes closed, I walked through the home imagining that it was years before. It smelled like geranium, like it always had. The nostalgia pulled at my heartstrings until my chest pooled like a deep, blue well. Tears welled in my eyes, and not because she was gone, but because all this time had passed. Those comfortable moments. Stepping back into Eva's home, I had expected to step right back into those days. But I had fallen into this sentimentality, and a longing for what was—a longing that, by the very nature of time, must go unfulfilled.

From her house, I took a photo album of polaroid pictures (none of which I was in), a pale blue box labeled *Archival Materials*, some figurines of the Virgin Mary, a bag of confetti, some blue marbles with the continents painted on them in orange, a few books, and a work Eva had written up and called *The Paradise Papers*, this being my favorite of all her madness. *The Paradise Papers* describe everyday normalcy, every mundane feature of living, every part of life that we walk blindly past every single day as if it were all the Garden of Eden itself. Eva appreciated life for exactly what it was; unromanticized, difficult, and mundane. Eva had no goals—she wanted nothing more out of life, she was so, so content and placated in her everyday magic.

I always planned on marrying Eva, to settle right into our routine for the rest of our days. This was a long time ago, when I had my corporate job, my pressed suits, and my shiny car, back when there was still hope that I would turn out to be the kind of young man a mother could be proud of. Way before I kneaded my fists into the walls of Eva's home and she sent all my worldly things flying out of her second-story window. My slumlord uncle, the type with a couple of bruises on his knuckles, too, was the only one to take pity on me.

I doubt Eva would have made a good wife. She devoted too much energy to her own little worlds, and so she had no interest in devoting herself to me, her future loving husband, her caretaker. I never knew what God she prayed to, but her bones were dense with piety. Her small breasts didn't fill her tops lewdly, never distracting from Eva's glowing heart. We didn't have sex in the last years, but she was going to be my wife, not my lover.

Lasciviousness is for the young, and sexual women end up in brothels, not at altars.

The day was falling to evening, and wet clouds bloomed like peonies in the sky. Periodically, they would tremble and open up salaciously, deluging the world below. Eventually, the wind blew them away, leaving nothing but midnight firmament and the perfect silk of an August night.

I sat by the window. A head full of wild, black curls came into view—a woman standing on the street, digging through her purse. She reminded me of my woman. She had pushed her curls back with a headset, its foam pads blasting into her ears. The wire of the headset worked its way down the front of her body, connecting to a CD player in her hand. She wore a pink, glittering bikini top and a white, spandex mini-skirt stretched over full hips and stomach rolls. She danced around in clear, Lucite stilettos. Staring at her own reflection in the windows of buildings, she rolled her hips, smirking at her own image, entranced by the sexuality of her own body. Absurd, and beautiful.

Every car that went by her honked furiously, like a dog barking for a slab of meat, their tongues hanging out of the window desperately. She ignored their hostile catcalls, their pathetic harassment, concerned only with herself. She continued her sensual dance, and I wished I could hear the song she was winding those hips to.

The woman picked wildflowers out of the overgrown lawn in front of my building. She ran her fingers through the simple daisies, harebells, and yarrow. Adorning her hair, she created a crown of cerulean forget-me-nots that glowed within her wreaths of curls. She threw fistfuls of glitter into the air and she sang aloud to the song which only she could hear—an absolute feral spectacle. My mouth hung open as I watched this crazy, immodest woman.

I wanted her, but she walked away and disappeared into the horizon of coming night.

She continued down my block, and I watched until I couldn't make out her form. I wanted to run after her; I wanted to fuck her in my checkered sheets. But the fledgling feathers on my forearms were growing in thickness and in number. They reminded me that sinful women meant trouble, much more trouble than their pleasures were worth. I laid down in bed alone. My heavy eyes, and my body aching for sleep…they overcame my motivation to do anything. I had an altar to create, this curse to break. But my body sunk deep into the down of the bed, and my own feathers lulled me into a warm state of relaxation. I slept a deep, dreamless sleep, falling farther and farther back into the blackness of unconsciousness.

SEVEN

Eva's home: a sanctuary for scavengers of all species. She was a lover of the living all her life, and in Eva's absence, a menagerie of creatures found their way into her abandoned residence. The slowest-moving beings made their way inside first. Ropes of violet clematis covered the entire facade, entwining with ivy vines and bindweed, squeezing the foundation into a creaking submission. Wild tangles of grasses overtook the entire yard and crept into every crevice and crack they could nestle into. Foxtails, dandelions, and Queen Anne's lace found their niches, too. The garden Eva had kept burst wild with flowers and true fruits. This liberation from the desecration that is modern landscaping allowed the yard to flourish green again, and soon, the creeping foliage and the arching branches of all these slow, living things overtook the entire house.

This was paradise for city bees who spent their numbered days buzzing from flower box to flower box. Caterpillars grew fat munching through all the luscious greenery, and in turn, little milky-white butterflies emerged, playing tag through the unkempt grass, and glorious monarchs soared through the clear air with their honey-colored warning stripes. Dedicated ants marched through their underground tunnels, as did so many other burrowing things. The weeds rustled not only in the wind but with the movements of all these tiny little creatures busy making this place into their home.

The birds had long eyed Eva's home from their perches high up in the messy trees, and it's possible that it was these very birds who told the trees to do it. Whatever their motivation, one day, the great, old, deciduous trees decided to shoot their emerald limbs right through the windowpanes of Eva's house. The birds chattered with glee, swooping down from their high nesting places, and hopped right down the low branches and into the house. It wasn't long before squirrels, chipmunks, and even raccoons followed suit. No one can remember when, but eventually, a short, storm-felled tree—and what it lacked in height, it made up in girth—crashed into the back of the house, and the heavy oak door, weakened by the multitude of living things that had been growing on and through it, caved in completely. Thus began a parade of life straight into the simple paradise of Eva's home.

There was the great egret who donned Eva's peach peignoir, a vision of ivory feathers coming down her long neck and into the sweet pink satin. Curious river turtles drew up soapy bubble baths, tilting an entire bottle of *Relaxing Milk & Honey Body Wash* into an overflowing tub. The finches, two and sometimes three at a time, heaved strings of pearls through the air, coiling them into nests within the bookshelves, and the sweet swallows nestled into clouds of pungent French perfume. Deer lounged on the loveseat and sofas, browsing among the cushions until the white stuffing came out. Titmice and other fowl scavenged the stuffing, carrying it into the cupboards and fixing their own fluffy nests inside teacups and cereal bowls. Cats lazed on the shelves above, eyeing the mice without menace or chase. Dogs tore through the house, yelping at the squirrels sheltered in the domesticized branches, and then barked their way into the bedroom, where they took deep, sleepy naps in Eva's flowered queen bed. Rats tore through notebooks and journals and boxes of losing lottery tickets, scattering them through the house and into their warm nesting places. Fire-tailed foxes nosed into unsecured cans of paint, choreographing their joyful prance and dancing all through the house with multicolored footprints. Creeping vines and butterflies lined the walls so thickly that they looked like wallpaper. Spiders, with their gossamer legs, netted every ceiling corner and open crevice in their sun-catching, silken webs.

Eva's sacred home, and the land upon which it had been built, was released from the social obligations of human inhabitants, returned to the lush and primitive.

EIGHT

I woke up late the next morning, still reeling from my experience at the brothel the night before and wishing, in my futile way, that it had all been a nightmare. My mouth ached with a stiff and painful jaw and my limbs pulsed, raw and prickling. I sat at the edge of my bed, and my neck started cocking forward uncontrollably. I tensed the muscles in my neck and shoulders, clenching the edge of my mattress until the avine seizures subsided.

I stumbled into the bathroom and threw my hands down on the sink. My heart in my stomach, I agonized over my own image; my body was feathered in soft ivory down. The feathers went up past my chin and down almost to the underside of my feet. Tawny feathers grew all the way up my neck and through my hair. My lips felt hard like cartilage, the flesh tinged a sickly yellow.

I moaned at my own image, tortured by this ridiculous curse. I started frantically plucking away at the feathers, desperate to reveal my human self. Painful tears ran down my cheeks and soaked into high-reaching feathers as I turned my skin bloody and raw. For every feather I plucked, two more sprouted in its place. My eyes welled with tears of pain, frustration, and fear. Blood and feathers spattered my floor until my bathroom looked like a butcher shop. I left the bathroom, closing the door behind me, as terrified of my own image as I'd been the night before.

My fear bubbled up into white, hot rage. Anger pooled into my veins, adding fire to a violence inside of me that I didn't altogether understand or even recognize. That bitch, Virgo, had taken away my humanity, and I had to *worship* her? I was supposed to go on like this apian whore was divine because she's powerful? She was a demon, and I would be doing men a service if I sent her straight to Hell. I could show up to the brothel with a gun, I thought; I was sure I wouldn't be the first. But, God, there would be a lot of witnesses. I could probably follow her home some night—beat her to death with my fists and make it look like a robbery. I'd break the curse for sure, and I'd probably make out with a few grand in cash. I wasn't sure I could do it, though, and she probably carried a gun—night women weren't stupid. They saw the true evil residing within us men. She might kill me first, and then I'd end up like that beheaded chicken.

I'm an idiot, I thought. It would be easier to swallow my pride and build the altar. I doubted I could actually kill someone anyway. I sat back down on my bed, the late morning sun shining pale onto my clean, new feathers covering damaged skin. I *was* an idiot. I got up and pulled on the jacket Maria had given me, zipping it up to hide my feathered neck. I pulled a hat down low over my feathered head and fished a pair of wool gloves out of my closet.

It was a hot day in August, but I could think of no other way to hide the curse.

I shoved my hands into my jacket pockets and found a twenty-dollar bill on the left side. I wondered if Maria had put it there, or if it had belonged to the jacket's owner. I grabbed a couple more crumpled twenty-dollar bills from under my mattress. I'd build this fucking altar here in my shitty apartment. I'd get everything she wanted from the thrift store. What did I need? A bunch of candles, all those flowers the old woman had mentioned, *forbidden fruit*…. Apples, I guessed.

That bitch Eve fucked us all over when she ate that infamous apple, kicking all of humanity out of the Garden and condemning us to this pointless, hopeless world.

Thick sheets of clouds iced the sky—smoothed out like a grocery store birthday cake, but lacking the cheer. I jumped on the Grand Avenue bus and headed east. The driver ignored my hello. It was midday, and the bus was almost empty. A pair of teenage lovers sat intertwined like vines in the back seat. I watched them, intrigued by their candidness and the impossibility of lovers. They sat side by side and folded their fingers together like feathers folding on the wings of a bird. The girl looked at her lover and her eyes bloomed like morning glories. She sat there, bubbling, and twirling her hair. He handsome, with dark features and full lips. He laughed at all her lame jokes and his face pulled into a genuine smile. I watched the girl beside him melt.

The bus rumbled up toward my stop, and I pulled the bell. Heading out the back door, I caught my last glimpse of the teenaged lovers locked into a sweet kiss before they both pulled away from each other blushing.

The thrift store was nestled under a viaduct at the end of a dead-end corridor. Eva had dragged me there all the time with her lectures about hope and purpose and giving used things a second *life*. She'd been fascinated by the lives of inanimate things and the stories she'd insisted were locked into their *essence*.

The store, rather dirty and unassuming, consisted of three creaky floors full of junk. Rusted shopping carts sat piled up in every corner. I headed downstairs to the basement, where they kept home goods and bric-a-brac. I moved through a sea of clutter—the offal of many, many people's lives, discarded and forgotten. We spend our lives constructing these worlds of material culture, only for it all to end up choked with dust in a basement somewhere, or in decay at the dump. Whatever meaning we've ascribed to our possessions, and the memories they kindled up inside of us, die with us. Eva, of course, disagreed. For her, objects had lives of their own; lives that didn't end with the death of their owners. Because of this belief, Eva made trips to the thrift store intolerable, and they always ended with her heartbroken and in tears over unloved teddy bears or abandoned wedding gifts.

I moved through the packed shelves, tempted to close my eyes like I had when I'd moved through Eva's cluttered home so many times and so long ago. I thought about all of the simple things that had made her happy, and how nothing about Virgo was simple. Yes, for Ms. Virgo, only the finest of thrift store finds would suffice.

For her, I chose a set of six, fine crystal champagne flutes perfect for casting refracted light, as well as twelve ivory pillar candles—each one with roses carved into its wax flesh—one lace tablecloth, adorned with embroidered wildflowers, that was perfect to set the altar, one garland of fake red roses, and one incense burner with bundles of *night-blooming jasmine* taped to the bottom, the embodiment of the Theater's air. I also found a Hawaiian-patterned shirt that someone had left among the glassware. I would never wear it, but I liked it, so I decided it would be mine. Down the aisle, a garden guidebook lay discarded atop a pile of women's blazers. I flipped through it before turning to the index. I searched the book for lavender, bee balm, and honeysuckle—flowers whose names I knew, but could not identify. I ripped their pictures out of the book and folded them into my pocket.

All of my careful choices filled a plastic handbasket that I carried gingerly to the register. The register sat on top of a scratched-up glass jewelry case. Within it, old watches and tacky costume jewelry clumped together in piles, stuck with age and dust. A nice old man rang me up. He grabbed the Hawaiian shirt and held it up to the light. He winked at me and said, "I have *the perfect* pair of pants that would go with this shirt."

I had no answer for this man who had the perfect pants to go with this gaudy shirt. He hummed to himself, taking his time packing my purchases into a single paper bag, rolling the glassware in newsprint. He read me my total, and I put the twenty-dollar bill I'd found in the jacket on the counter. The man's eyes lingered on my gloved hands for a moment before he picked up the money. The register rang and slid open with a thud. Counting my change out carefully, he reached out to hand it to me. I busied my hands as best I could in the pockets of my jacket, hoping he wouldn't ask why I was wearing mittens in the depths of summer. Calmly, he waited. Finally, I awkwardly told him to leave the change on the counter. Frowning, he obliged and turned back to my bag. I swiped up the money quickly and grabbed the bag's flimsy paper handle. The bag pulled heavily towards the ground, so I instead held it in my arms, close to my chest. As I turned to leave, I caught a glance at the Hawaiian shirt that I would never wear resting at the top of the bag. I pulled it out and laid it back on the counter.

"I don't own anything that would look good with this."

The man smiled his crinkly smile, and I turned and walked out the door.

I waited fifteen minutes before the bus came, the heavy paper bag resting on the ground, and I shifted my itchy feathered feet. When the bus finally came, I took a seat toward the front. A kid with bubble-gum pink shoes and a skateboard took up an entire two seats across from me. He stared down at my feet. I looked down to see that tawny, feathered ankles stuck out from underneath the hem of my pants, pulled upward from sitting. My face burned crimson and I twisted awkwardly, trying to leverage my pant legs lower.

When my stop came, I rang the bell and stood to exit. The kid looked up at me and said, "Cool socks." I hustled off the bus, gloved hands fumbling for my keys. I left my shopping bag upstairs and headed three blocks west so that I could buy the forbidden fruit. There, men sat along the sidewalk in checkered folding chairs. They sold fruit at the intersection from the trailer of their pickup truck. Apples, pears, peaches, and plums cascaded down from cardboard boxes, filling the rusted-out truck so that it resembled a jewel box. I chose a bag of apples that still had leaves attached to the stems. They didn't gleam like waxed supermarket apples, and they didn't need that artificial coating to look delicious. The men asked for three dollars for the entire bag, and I handed them three crumpled bills from my gloved hand. They didn't bat an eye at my attire. They, too, wore long sleeves and had hats pulled down low, protecting their skin from a long day of sitting outside in the sun.

I was almost at Marmora Avenue, so I decided to stop by Eva's old yard and see if the flowers I needed were growing there. The great, overgrown site was unrecognizable in its state of wild disarray. Her beautiful house was just a shell of broken windows and overgrown weeds. I felt none of the nostalgia I had expected. This was not the home I had known.

A narrow path divided Eva's fence from the trees that lined train tracks. I followed it to the back gate, which I wrenched open despite its years of disuse and the vines that grew all over its hinges. It squealed as if it had forgotten its purpose and protested my invasion of its quiet autonomy. As I tramped through Eva's yard, flocks of birds lifted into the air like giant, cawing clouds. I rustled through beds of weeds until I saw purple buds of lavender and the wild heads of bee balm stalks. I grabbed a handful of the stalks and used my keys to slice at the woody stems. The birds screamed at me from the trees like *I* was the intruder in this space where I had once lived. I pulled at the flowers, ripping them from the ground, and the birds swooped low at my head in protest. Dodging their razor claws, I fought my way back to the other side of the gate, and it squeaked shut as I headed home all covered in leaves and nettles.

The stoop of my building was covered in the honeyed light of the end of day. I sat down on a step and started to pull burrs from my feathered ankles. I looked at the field across the street, and at all the low-growing things that the property manager tried desperately to tame. I crossed over and laced my fingers through the chain link. Standing there, I pulled out the picture of honeysuckle that I had stolen from the thrift store and searched through the field, which was much less dense than Eva's yard. Curling up at the base of a great tree, the small, tiny dancers inside honeysuckle blooms twirled through fawn grass. The chain link was old and pliable. I was able to lift the bottom up like a skirt and grab the honeysuckle by the stems. Fruity and pungent, the honeysuckle petals continued their ballet as if they had not been disturbed at all.

Back in the privacy of my apartment, I spent time examining the progression of my vicious, avian transformation. When I was sufficiently repulsed by my own appearance, I turned my attention to the offerings that lay in bags on my kitchen floor. I had wrapped the flowers all in bundles of brown paper and twine, hoping to preserve them for the night. A wooden chest of drawers leaned against my living room wall, and I closeted the knickknacks that lived out their lives pooling dust. Wiping the top down with my sleeve, I watched as its old luster came back. The tablecloth fit inelegantly on the oblong wardrobe, and I hid the creased fabric with the full orbs of everlasting rose garland. I juxtaposed the lit pillar candles with half-filled champagne flutes so that the flames wiggled through the crystal, casting rainbows all over the table and floor. The apples, I kept in their paper bag and set on the table, next to the floral packages. Sticks of jasmine incense slid out of their cardboard package, and I lit one, wafting it over the altar.

I laid the phone book out on my kitchen table. I had never ordered a house call before, but I'd seen signs advertising *Seductive Nights in the Comfort of One's Own Home* in the bathrooms of the Theater. To me, the Theater was a great museum. Not only did huge static canvasses line the walls, but a living diversity of women, each a work of art in their own existence, painted themselves through the lavender rooms. There, sex was art, and the women's companionship was worth the premium price. But here? In my shitty apartment?

I circled the Theater's listing and dialed the number on my phone, anxiously twisting the cord. Someone picked up on the first ring. A woman with a monotone voice, aloof and obviously uninterested, answered, "The Theater...."

I hesitated, expecting her to go on.

"*Hello?*" she asked, without any change in the intonation of her voice.

"Yeah, hi!" I spat out quickly. "I'm, uh, I'm looking for a house call." I heard the rustle of paper from the other end of the line.

"What kind of girl you looking for?" she asked flatly.

Scratching at my feathers, I said, "I want Virgo."

The rustling stopped. She was silent for a moment, and then she replied, "Virgo doesn't do house calls."

I nestled my face into my palm. Of course, she didn't.

"I'm her regular." I said.

"Virgo doesn't do house calls," she said again, without the slightest shift in tone.

"I'll pay whatever it takes." I pleaded.

"No means no," she responded apathetically, and no amount of begging would change her mind.

Exasperated, I yelled into the phone, "I don't even want to fuck her! I just need her to break this goddamn curse!"

Silence, and then: "Well, why didn't you just say so?"

I heard paper rustling on the other end. The woman took down my name, address, and phone number.

"You better have at least $500 in cash…as in, minimum."

She hung up the phone. I had exactly $500, which I had planned on putting towards rent, but people make plans and God laughs. And just like that, Virgo, this demon who was ruining my life, would be waltzing into my apartment. My stomach curled into knots and my palms dampened with sweat at the thought.

NINE

It was evening, and the four o'clocks had long wilted for their night's sleep. I stood by the window, an anxious eye on a street illuminated only by the marigold glow of streetlights and a white moon. My stomach undulated, queasy with butterflies, and I bit at my nails, which became more osseous and claw-like by the hour. I had on a clean shirt and a clean pair of trousers; I'd even managed to get the dirt spots out of my sneakers. I looked all right.

As the time of the goddess's arrival neared, I became more finicky about my feathers. I caught myself preening my forearms against my cheeks, then fluffing them out and preening them back down again. Cartilage continued to spread through my lips—painfully—deepening in yellow.

My doorbell rang and I nearly jumped out of my skin. I hadn't seen her approach my building, and my unaware heart, suddenly very conscious of its own responsibility to beat, pounded hot blood into my weakened legs. I steadied my dizzy steps with a palm on the table and crept toward the buzzer. I paused at the door with my hand gripping the brass knob, hesitant to let this volatile whore into my home. However, our goddess was an impatient one, and again, the buzzer screamed out. I held down my own buzzer, unlocking the downstairs door with a hum.

I heard the piteous heave of the great, old door and a series of dainty taps, followed by a sympathetic release as the door slammed shut like a tired old man falling back into his worn, leather recliner. Then, *tap, tap, tap, tap, tap, tap,* like tiny raindrops spotting onto a windowpane. *Tap, tap, tap,* all the way up the stairs. *Tap, tap, tap,* down the hall, and then silence outside my door.

I held my breath. There came no knock; instead, a pink waft of smoke squeezed itself underneath my door, perfumed like fresh-cut peonies in June. The cloud inched itself in, filling in along the floor and carpeting the entire room.

I backed away from this encroaching cloud until I hit the bed. I sat at the edge with my fingers gripping my mattress, bracing for whatever was to come. The door, as if unaffixed by locks or even doorknobs, opened like a butterfly's wing, without its habitual creaking and with a voluptuousness that resembled the swing of a full woman's curving hip. More pink clouds and sweet florals filled the doorway dramatically. I was sitting on the beach, looking out into this sugared sunset which filled in all of the blue of the sky, until darkness vined its way across the horizon, leaving nothing but cover for sinners and a splatter of stars under which young lovers kissed.

Tap, tap, tap, again, and the darkness crept into my room. Virgo: the definition of sensuality. She was wrapped into a tight, cheetah-print dress—a hooker classic. Her breasts sat high within the cups of the dress, testing the strength of its spaghetti straps. That black hair, which had disturbed me to the point of madness during our first encounter, was neither smart nor neat, and instead hung all around her in thick waves.

I swallowed hard as the surplus of blood that my heart had pumped out headed for my cock. I thrust my hands into my pockets in a futile attempt to conceal my erection. Virgo was sexual, all womanhood and femininity. Her legs—*God, those legs*—walked toward me in a pair of sparkling stilettos. She *tap, tap, tapped* her way over to where I sat and straddled me on the bed. Leaning into me, she crooned, "Let's get the financials out of the way, so we can have some fun."

Did she even recognize me? Surely, the woman on the phone had told her the reason for the house call. How many of us had she gotten to?

Grasping at my wallet, I pulled my feathered hands out of my pocket. I held my wallet in the narrow space between her large breasts and my sullen chest. Virgo let silence fill in between us. She raised her eyebrows at the sight of my hands, and then turned her eyes up to my face, at which point her brow came to a resting furrow. She stepped down from the bed and crossed her arms in front of me.

"You," she said quietly.

I held my hands up in surrender, my wallet still in hand. The sleeves of my shirt slid down, revealing more down feathers.

"Please…" I began.

"Fuck you," she replied with force.

She turned on her heel and grabbed her coat, reaching for the door. I sprang up and screamed for her to stay. I launched myself forward, using the momentum of my entire body to close the door she had only barely opened.

"You can't leave!"

Virgo took a step back. "I can do whatever the fuck I want!" She pulled a small, silver pistol out of the breast pocket of her coat and pointed it at my panicked face.

Again, I raised my hands in a silent plea for mercy. "Please," I tried again, "please, *Goddess*."

She raised an eyebrow, though the gun kept steady, aimed at my forehead.

I continued, "I called for you only to try and make amends. I was so wrong. I brought you here to make things right. Didn't they tell you what I said when I made the appointment?!"

Virgo did not lower the gun. She said nothing.

I continued, "I went to see the woman in the alley off Marmora Avenue. She told me how to do your ritual—I want to make things right!" I held out a feathered hand, hoping she would take it. She did not.

"How to *do* my ritual." She muttered.

"Please, Virgo...look!"

I made my way to the makeshift altar, daring myself to breathe with that pistol undoubtedly aimed at the back of my head. Virgo followed in her shoes that cost more than my entire apartment.

I pulled a long-stemmed match from the box that sat on my kitchen table and struck it until it burned with flame. I lit the altar candles, and they glowed against Virgo's pretty face. She made no attempt to hide her amusement.

"What is this?" she asked.

"The altar," I answered, confused. "The lady told me I needed to make you an altar."

Virgo responded with a stream of laughter, one so heartening that she lowered her gun and stuffed it into her purse. She came closer to examine the altar I'd spent all afternoon perfecting, which she now ridiculed silently. When she finished her inspection, she turned around to face me. Virgo leaned against the altar so that both her palms pressed down on the tablecloth, one covering a blue forget-me-not while the other hid half of a magnolia.

"This," she began, "is hilarious."

That familiar flame of anger ignited inside me. I'd put in all this effort for *her*.

"This is *very* misguided," she concluded.

I didn't understand. "What are you talking about?" I asked, audibly frustrated. "I did everything that woman told me to, I got everything, I even—"

Virgo put a finger to her lips, ending my pathetic griping.

A sly smile spread across her cherry red lips.

"So, tell me, what did the woman tell you to do *exactly*?" she asked.

What a dumb question. Wasn't it obvious?

"She told me I had to pray to your altar."

Again, she giggled. "This," she threw a thumb behind her shoulder, motioning to my pitiful attempt at a sacred ritual, "is *not* the altar of Virgo." She ran her hands all up and down her body, lasciviously. "*I* am the altar."

She threw her hands up in the air, cocking out a hip—all smiles, chin up and eyes closed.

"Bring me my money," Virgo ordered. Her fingers shuffled through the cash like a machine. She shoved my payment deep into her purse and took out a brown envelope. Then she began to undress. I shifted my eyes around nervously, unsure of what the hell was going on, what she expected, and whether I would end up a headless chicken or not. Standing in mauve lingerie, Virgo took my avian hand and said, "I will teach you the ritual, and if you do it right, I will allow you to pray to the altar of me." She dropped my hand and walked toward the bathroom, her swinging hips beckoning me to follow.

Shuffling through the bloody feathers still stuck to my bathroom floor, I fully expected sex.

Virgo turned toward me with a frown. "Where are my offerings?"

Here we go, I thought. I went out to the altar, the one Virgo had insisted was not an altar, and grabbed the flowers, the fruit, a paring knife, and the cheap body wash, and turned back into Virgo's den of iniquity.

Virgo perched on the closed toilet. She had one leg crossed over the other, and sat tall and regal. She looked so out of place in the shitty bathroom, though the blue glow of night cast a pretty color over the image of her. I laid everything I carried in my arms on the floor next to her.

Virgo began the ritual. "First," she said, "you draw the bath." She took the bubble bath from my hands and cradled it like a child. "I would have thought that part was the most obvious."

Eyes rolling, I knelt beside the tub and fingered the rusted chain of the rubber stopper. I plugged the tub and unscrewed the white plastic cap of the bubble bath bottle. Running the water very warm, I poured in a generous amount of bubble bath. Virgo, looking over my shoulder, tilted the bottle in my hands, pouring its entire contents into the water.

The bubble bath filled the room with an aroma that was neither milk nor honey. This scent…I couldn't place it in this world; it was Aphrodite's perfume. Bubbles erupted from the tub like delicate diamond mines, iridescent in the moonlight. Still seated on her porcelain throne, Virgo handed me the brown envelope.

"Now this," she whispered, as if she were being careful not to scare its contents away.

I opened the envelope; it was just a bunch of dried flowers. *Pretty mundane for some sex goddess*, I thought. I scattered them over the bath and purple pansies came to rest on the mountains of bubbles, their yellow hearts bursting from their centers. They looked like little angels sitting in the clouds of Heaven.

Virgo and I sat in silence as the water filled. She sat on the toilet smirking at my feathers, and I squirmed anxiously in the doorway. Bubbles erupted all over the sides of the clawfoot tub and overflowed onto the pink-tiled floor. They glistened and murmured, and Virgo slumped closer to listen. Rising, she stepped both her dainty little feet into the soapy brew. She pulled up her hair, tied it on top of her head, and then sank into the bath like a flooded ship.

Her eyes closed in recline, she kept silent and still. Had she fallen asleep? I maintained my post of anxiety at the doorway, worry chewing at my insides as feathers and bird features clawing at my outsides. Eventually, I took Virgo's place on the toilet, quietly and with the composure of calmness—afraid to anger her, or scare her away from the beginnings of her peace.

I looked around at my own bathroom, trying to occupy my mind away from this lunacy that had become my life. My eyes darted around the tears in the wallpaper and the mildew stains, bouncing all around all these ugly things, not daring to look at Virgo.

When my curiosity overcame me, I took a glance at this eccentric woman in my tub. One eye was open and focused on me. She raised her eyebrow when our eyes met, and said, "So, are you going to do the ritual or are you gonna keep examining your walls?"

I jumped up, feeling foolish.

"Yeah!" I exclaimed with a ridiculous enthusiasm. "I'm supposed to, uh, feed you the fruit, and then, um, something with the flowers?"

She reached both her hands out of the water and put them behind her head, reclining further. "Start with the fruit," she said calmly.

Apples streaked with the dying colors of fall glistened from a brown paper bag. I chose one and ran the knife through the middle of the apple, separating it at the heart. I carved out the seeds and core, leaving only the unfertile flesh and skin behind. I quartered the apples and halved each quarter, arranging the slices on a pink, glass plate neatly, like a flower. I left the browning discards in the paper they'd come in, and held the plate up for Virgo to see.

Virgo sat in the tub, just a head in a sea of bubbles. She looked at me, her red lips not pulled into a smirk but a little smile.

"Apples?" she asked.

"Forbidden fruit," I replied simply.

"There are no apples in the garden," she declared, as if she had been there.

Virgo rose from the foaming bath and the water fell around her like a silk robe, bubbles streaming down like lace with the dim light from the bathroom window catching her body like irised silk ribbons. She stepped out one dainty foot at a time, and tiptoed into the living room as if in Cinderella's glass slippers, her wet, silk ribbons trailing behind her.

I stepped into the doorway, following her wet tracks through my apartment. Virgo knelt at the base of an old, neglected ficus plant I kept by the window. The previous tenants had left it behind. So, it lived, modestly, here in the hazy light of my home. Virgo caressed its branches with tenderness; she whispered into the creases of its leaves. My ficus stroked her cheeks with its emerald fronds, bowed to Virgo, and she knelt at its confined, compacted roots. Every one of its stalks hunched together, its leaves folding like a prayer. Virgo now bowed her head as the ficus grew a mass in its green heart, and bore a single fruit which Virgo cradled in her hands and pulled away from the vine. She held the fruit to her heart, as it ripened into a deep orange, and the ficus reached towards the ceiling, heralding its place in some divine plan.

I sat back down as Virgo reappeared in the doorway—flushed and grinning. A persimmon sat in her hands and her purse hung at her elbow. The pearl handle of her pistol peeked from the mouth of her bag. The deep orange-fleshed persimmon looked perfectly ripe, without even a hint of jaundice. I took it in my hands, held it up to my nose, and inhaled deeply. I wanted to bite deep into its fleshy fruit, feel inside it with my tongue and slurp out its juices. I wanted it for myself, but Virgo would eat it all, without any concern for my desire or needs. She wouldn't share this fruit with me, and I was angry with her for not indulging me with her fruit.

"How is this possible?" I asked.

"Paradise is in the here and now."

The white flesh of the apple had started to soften and brown. I slid it off the plate and back into the brown paper bag. Virgo sank back into the water as I sat with the plate in my lap, coring the persimmon and slicing it. As each sliver slipped from the steel of the knife, desire bloomed inside of me, arousal flaming in the core of my stomach. I held up the knife and watched the pale orange juice sliding down its blade and over my fingers. My eyes then focused on Virgo in the bath, her red lips raging. The wax of her lipstick had faded away, but her lips were still stained. They parted, and she stuck her tongue out, as if to say she was ready to be fed.

The itch of feathers on my skin jolted me away from this sweet, orange fantasy. I knelt next to the tub. Virgo sat up, her breasts emerging from the water covered in suds, her eyes half-masked and pink in her cheeks. I took a slice of forbidden fruit between two fingers and steadied her face with my hand at her cheek. I touched the fruit to her stained lips until they glistened with nectar. They parted, and she stuck out her tongue to taste the persimmon flesh, sucking the slice into her mouth and then swallowing it whole as if she were a snake. I grimaced, and she smirked at my discomfort. The next persimmon slice melted ripe and luscious in her mouth. She chewed the pulp and skin, her mouth sticky with sweetness.

We sat together, she draped over the side of the tub like fabric and I cross-legged on the bathroom floor. Every bite burst with sun, though the sun hadn't ripened this fruit. I fed her slice after slice, until the feathers on my hands turned orange and Virgo's tongue was dyed sunset.

Virgo pulled her knees into her chest, wrapping her arms around her shins and hunching her shoulders. She took a deep, sighing breath of satiation. Pansies stuck to her skin, and I pictured vines growing all up and down her fertile body—an earth to the sacred, the beautiful, the unappreciated and rejected. Her body glowed in the moonlight that had crept in through the small shower window. The water hadn't cooled at all, as her hot, glowing heart radiated throughout the entire room. She was a beautiful, magical thing, and how could I have hated something so wondrous? How could I have been so threatened by such a creature like her? But in this moment, she was no creature. I saw no bees, or felines, or any animal besides human. This woman was full and gentle, even vulnerable, though my own body still held the scars of her strength.

"Now," she whispered, in a lucid state of calm, "bring me the flowers."

"And I braid them into your hair?" I blurted out.

Virgo, her cheek now resting on top of her knees, cracked a little smile. "Good boy," she murmured.

I reached for the brown-papered packages of flowers. She let down her long hair, and it hung down her back. The ends swirled in the bathwater—brushing leftover bubbles aside, catching a flower here and there. I carefully opened each package, sweet pollen dusting from the paper.

"Lavender, bee balm, and honeysuckle," I recited.

Virgo smiled her sleepy smile. "Very good."

The rich, herbal scent of lavender flora clouded the room as I pulled away the paper. I laid out each flower on the tile floor. Virgo's eyes were closed, and she breathed deeply.

My unskilled hands fumbled through her damp hair. I took a section, dividing it into three sleek pieces in my hands, laid the lavender down between the hair, and began to knit it all together. The plaits hung unevenly, but I continued. I grabbed stems of orange honeysuckle, drawing them up to her hair and braiding them all together.

I worked like this for a long time, piece by piece, in my silent worship of this woman. When all of the hair was sectioned and done with flowers, I craned my neck and peered into her face. She opened her eyes and peered right back at me.

"Are you done now?" she questioned softly.

"Yes," I replied.

She let go of her knees and sat cross-legged in the bath. She gently touched her braids, feeling the novice awareness of my fingers through each course plait, though she said nothing. She began to pull each braid above her head and around her hairline.

"Get some pins out of my purse," she instructed me.

I leaned over to her purse, which sat on the toilet. My hand pushed past the gun as I reached for a piece of cardboard to which she had clipped several bobby pins. I handed them to her one by one, and she pushed them into her hair. Her dark hair, dotted with specks of purple and orange, sat all tied up into a regal crown. Her eyes still closed, she held her head high, shoulders back. Bathwater lapped at her skin, that glowing heart brighter than the full moon.

A goddess sat in my tub. This worship was simple; easy, delicate. In participating in this ritual, I felt that I had started the healing of my own soul, atoning for my sins against this woman, and Eva, and all women who I had ever felt dominion over. Softhearted people are never easy, and I'd learned that with Eva. But in this moment, my heart softened, too, and I started to feel more human than beast.

Virgo sat back in the tub and again reclined. She sat low in the water and propped her feet on the opposite side of the tub—my cue for the next ritual. I grabbed the bee balm and touched the petals to the bottoms of her feet.

She opened one eye. "You have to make a paste," she said sleepily.

"A paste?" I questioned.

"Crush up the petals in a bowl." That, her only instruction.

I retrieved a small bowl from the kitchen and came back to sit on the bathroom floor. I plucked all of the petals from each stem, and with my fingers, I firmly pressed and rubbed them into the bottom of the bowl until eventually a substance redolent of crimson paste formed.

I took a good helping of the bee balm, fragrant and sweet, and rubbed it into the arches of Virgo's pedicured feet. Working it in with my thumbs, I moved from the ball of each foot outward, in the shape of a fanning scallop shell, the white of my feathers staining maroon and blue. There I was at her feet as she mewed and sighed. After I spent significant time on each foot, I dipped them back into the bath, washing off my homemade paste. Now, Virgo was bathed, fed, and pampered. She had to break the curse.

I dipped my feathered hands into the water as she submerged herself completely, displacing this small body of water we'd created together. I stood and dried my hands on an old embroidered hand towel. The room creaked in silence; the bath water lilted. I could hardly see Virgo under the sea of plant debris and leftover suds. I waited for her to come up for air, leaning over the tub, the water reflecting my own image back to me like some primitive mirror. Feathers crept up my jawline, nestling into the hallows of my cheeks as if they belonged. Anger leapt inside of me, and I suddenly imagined reaching into that tub and holding her under the water. But then Virgo emerged, softened and new, flowers clinging to her like vernix, and the bubble bath foam glistened on her skin like lanugo.

She wrapped her arms around herself and batted her eyelashes like a sleepy doe. Reaching into her crown, Virgo started to pluck out all of the pins she had carefully placed and to shake out the braids and flowers entangled in them. All of my clumsy work, she had undone. She stood, and water dripped from her figure like shooting stars crashing from the sky, her hair curling all around her, heavy and dark. I pulled a bath towel off its hook and offered it to Virgo. She accepted this perfectly mundane offering and tucked herself into it.

"I need one for my hair," she said, so I pulled the other towel down and watched as she flung her dark curls over her head and into the towel. She stepped out of the bath, still glistening, and I followed her out of the room.

Virgo stood in front of the altar I had put together for her. This time, she wasn't laughing at my rudimentary sense of devotion. I had never worshiped any woman, but Virgo excited me—the way she dressed, her absurd rituals, the pistol tucked into her purse. I wanted her.

She sat on my bed, toweling her legs dry. I sat next to her awkwardly.

She said, "Pretty good job."

I smiled at her, ready to try my luck without the Queen of Hearts in my pocket.

"You're beautiful," I told her. "I was way out of line to talk to a beautiful woman like you the way I did."

Her eyebrows furrowed with suspicion. "You'd be out of line to talk to *any* woman like that. What does beauty have to do with it?"

"Because," I started, "you're different from other women. I don't even know you, and I can tell that you demand a different kind of respect. I like that in a woman. How many women can call themselves goddesses, and actually get someone to treat them like it?" I ended my statement with a small string of laughter, expecting her to be flattered by my words; however, her face folded stoically.

She spoke clearly, cold and direct, "I don't call myself a goddess; I am a goddess. Divinity is a part of womanhood, and I identify as a woman. I don't reside outside of sisterhood with other women, and I don't reside within a competition with other women. What you like within a woman is irrelevant, and how you define a woman is irrelevant. You define these boundaries of womanhood as breasts and bearing children…anatomy and emotionality…. Is that because it distracts you from acknowledging the femininity inside yourself?"

She didn't need my approval, but her entire career centered around the desires of men—men finding her beautiful, men wanting to fuck her. I told her this as delicately as I could, trying to get her to understand that, without men like me, there would be no her. She shook her head at every single word of my rebuttal and asked, "My life is centered around men? How much money have you spent at the Theater? Did I go out and find you, or did you walk into *my* workplace, night after night? To me, you're just a client, but to you, I am so much more."

"I'm just a customer, but you need my money." That was my pitiful counter-argument.

"I don't *need* your money, I *want* it. Did it ever occur to you that I actually enjoy this work?"

Virgo slid on her garter and rolled up her stockings, clipping them into place. Silently, she continued dressing, brow furrowed. Then, "I know you want me to break the curse."

I nodded. "Please, Virgo."

She stood up, hand on hip, frowning. She sighed and bowed her head. "But what will it take for men to see us as we are?"

I stood and approached her. I lifted her chin with one finger, till her eyes met mine. "I see you," I said, and then I leaned into her, pulling her face up into a kiss. But she pulled back violently, grabbed my arms, and pushed me away with such force that I fell back onto the bed.

"What the hell are you doing?!" she asked incredulously.

I stood and tried to grab her by the waist. She twisted away and slapped me clean across the face, seething.

"Look," I started, "you're a beautiful woman, and you don't have to play hard to get because I already had you, and you just said you enjoy the work right?"

I smirked up at her horrified face.

But this, evidently, had been the wrong thing to say. Without words, Virgo squared her whole body in front of mine, and swiftly snapped her wrists, then fingers, into the air. An audible *crack* rang out from somewhere deep inside of me, followed by entire, searing, corporal pain. I dropped to my knees screaming. Feather after feather exploded out of my skin. My joints crunched and stiffened, and my ribs squeezed my organs together, compacting my whole human body together as my spine bent and twisted in unnatural angles. My eyes bleary with tears, I clawed at the feathers, ripping them out, only adding to my suffering.

Virgo laughed maniacally, though I could barely hear it over my own screams.

"You did not learn your lesson, young man," she crooned cheerily.

"Virgo, please…" I begged in between gasps.

Her response was laughter.

"You can't do this to me!"

She walked right past my writhing body and straight for the door. Designer bag in hand, Virgo reached for the knob.

I could not let her leave.

I thrust my arm out, and my bones sounded like shattered glass. I grabbed her ankle, pulled her to the ground, and dragged her back. With my other hand, I reached for her bag. She yanked her arm forward as hard as she could—scrambling to get up on her knees, scrambling to control the bag. I could feel the leather stretch, then the handle laced around her arm snapped and the bag came flying back toward me. I let go of her ankle and fumbled inside the bag, searching for the gun, my mangled body devoid of coordination. Virgo, regaining some balance, leapt on top of me, desperate for the weapon.

My hand groped the cool, metal barrel, and my fingers fumbled for the handle. I was blind with pain, gasping for air, and Virgo punched me as hard as she could—so hard that I could taste blood. She grabbed my wrists, attempting to tilt them away from her person, but my finger wrapped around the trigger and the gun went off. I laid down as the chaos in my body immediately began to calm. My arms and legs started to lengthen, the bones mending back together, my joints loosening, chest expanding. Waves of cool covered my entire body like a milk bath soothing poxed skin. I heard the door open, and the shuffling of feet into the hallway, and then the rapid tapping of heels all down the stairs. When I opened my eyes, loose feathers reddened with blood covered me like snowfall. I sat up and the feathers all fell away. I realized the blood was not my own. Virgo's purse still hung clenched in my fist, and a clean bullet hole burned through the bottom, its entire face splattered with blood.

Blood marbled all over my floor, a bloody handprint covered the door handle, and drops of blood spotted all over the stairs. I heard the building's heavy entry door slam shut and I ran to the window. Virgo stumbled out of my building and across the street. Clutching the fence that enclosed the stretch of fields, she held herself up with one hand while her other clutched at her chest. From a distance, it looked like ink was seeping through her fingers. She careened forward to the gap in the fence—the same gap that I had seen the big black dog cross through on the last morning of his life. Virgo, now on her hands and knees, crawled through that same space, collapsed on the other side, and did not move again.

TEN

I am the Honey Goddess—the goddess of sweetness, love, and tender care. I am a flowering and dying goddess who sits in both life and death, and distinguishes little in between. My love is sacred divination, and my heart dispels loneliness in the hearts of the troubled. I am Virgo, the cannon of soft pleasure, the ruler of cosmic passion, and the pleasure of the Divine.

A fever dream: I leaned against a rusty old fence and took my hand away from my wound. Blood wreathed around my fingers and pulled away in strings like thick spiderweb. It ran down my body—away from the bullet, over my breasts, staining my satin bra. I was not afraid.

My stilettos made it difficult to cross the field, but they sparkled in moonlight, reminiscent of stars, and it was too beautiful to end. I made my way to the sacred threshold; a journey I had not made before, a journey of intuition. I was so very close, but I had lost so much blood, and my legs trembled, too weak to stand. I dropped to my knees and began to crawl.

I'd been wrong in my judgment of that man. He deserved the curse, and he wasn't worthy to worship at the altar of any woman, especially not a goddess of the gentle. But that was neither here nor there now.

The threshold emanated warmth and light. I passed through. I collapsed safely on the other side, waiting for Eden to call. I always had passion for the Garden. I rested my cheek on the grass, crisp with night, and through a space between the dilapidated apartment buildings, I could see the sky. It twinkled with midnight and infinite stars, and I twinkled back, resonant and good. I closed my eyes.

The breeze was full of the sweet scent of peony trees and the earthiness of greens; I was being pulled through a forest, pulled up into the air. I looked down at my sparkling shoes, and flowers fell all around me. I flew through the night, someone clutching at my underarms, and heard the rustle of…feathers? I watched through sleepy eyes, like a long dream. I flew high above ground, but lower than the mother lark whose wings swept over me like a blessing until I arrived at a riverbank.

I fluttered over the water, straight to its heart, and I dropped lower and lower. Soon, I was in the river, and my shoes slid off my feet and sank into the water. I, too, was sinking, and slowly, I submerged, the last of the August-silk night slipping away. The blood from my wound surrounding me like a gown. I did not breathe, and I did not feel the urge to. Wildfowl flew overhead, no doubt eyeing the fish swimming past my ankles and through my fingers. I opened my eyes. Above the water, I could see the beginnings of a honey sky, flushing like the afterglow of an orgasm…the opening of the threshold that kept apart the living and the dead. The early bright of morning was rushing in. I sank away from the daybreak.

Sank lower into the tide,
    down,
        down.
Away from the threshold.
Into the night of deep water.

ELEVEN

I pressed my forehead to the windowpane and tried to envision steam rising from the demon I had slayed. While I thought my task had been to appease the witch, what had ultimately dispelled the curse was her destruction. Had she ever even intended to break the curse, a vindictive woman like her? Now, she laid in the field on the other side of the fence, her satin lingerie reflecting the moon. Fireflies lit up like falling stars all around her.

I closed the curtains and sat on the edge of my bed—waiting for sirens, waiting for *something*. Surely, someone had heard the gun go off, or seen a half-naked woman run across the barren street into the unkempt grass.

There was no sound, there was nothing.

Eventually, I willed myself back into the bathroom and filled a bucket up with warm, soapy water. Virgo's blood, which had lost its sheen as it oxidized and dried, came up easily under the grain of my sponge. The bucket clattered loudly every time I moved it to a different spot on the floor, seemingly louder than the sound of the gun. Still, I continued, my shaking hands wringing out the yellow sponge. I made my way down the stairs, imagining how it would look if one of my neighbors walked out of their apartment and saw me doubled over, washing blood off the stairs. But the building was silent, making my every movement deafening.

Back in my apartment, I started sweeping up all of the feathers I had shed. Not even an hour had passed, but the feathers had shriveled—their pure white dulled, muddied even. They disintegrated into ash with each stroke of the broom.

I turned my attention to the altar and tore it apart, throwing all that I had so carefully curated into a cardboard box. The tub was a massacre of flowers, with pansies clinging to the sides in purple and yellow streaks. Petals and leaves clogged the drain, leaving inches of bathwater without escape. The whole room reeked of earth and green and lavender.

I cleaned the drained tub of all natural matter and then scrubbed it. I used Virgo's towel to dry the floor then threw them into the box too. I went through her purse, grabbing the money I had paid her as well as several hundred dollars she'd also had. I slid her handgun under my mattress.

When I had sufficiently returned my apartment to the state of chaos that I'd enjoyed before Virgo had ever set foot inside, I turned my attention back to the window. Heavy drawn curtains protected my inside world from light and reality, like dark clouds blown over a sunny day or a solar eclipse—the end of the world. The light from the street seeped in at the corners of the curtains, swirling with dust.

I took hold of the fabric and pulled it toward me, allowing light in while still preventing me from seeing outside. Eventually, my curiosity overcame my fear and I yanked the curtain aside, exposing the full night, the empty street, and an empty lot. Virgo was not there.

Relief and horror crashed over me simultaneously. Her absence surely meant that she had found the strength to leave. There had been no sirens. If she lived, she would try to curse me again, especially after this night.

I grabbed the gun from under the mattress and tucked it into my waistband and walked out the door. I descended the stairs, wafting through the fresh scent of cleaning solution. I pulled open the heavy entry door and walked out onto my stoop. The night was a calm and quiet film covered the world that only the wind disturbed. The wind picked up, and with it came the fallen leaves and detritus of late summer. They came together in the air and took on the shape of a woman. The empty space of the night was full of her hips and the tangling of her hair. Petals and pollen curved around the slight of her waist, her breasts, and up her rounding shoulders and length of neck. This woman passed through the night—her voice the rustle of leaves, the stirring of litter and cans, the creak of tree branches.

I crossed the street just as Virgo had, passing through the wind with its hands rustling in my hair, blustering at my shirt. I came to the field where I had seen Virgo come to rest, and the grass I had seen her stumble through seemed undisturbed. I followed her path, my own footsteps crunching through the foliage, leaving deep-set footprints in the earth. I followed close to the neighbor girl's apartment. Her open windows glowed pink with string lights. Soft music emanated from her room, and I willed it to hide the disaster of my footsteps.

I continued down Virgo's tragic path, and as the clouds cleared the moon, its light shone down on me in the field, leaving me exposed to the black night and the crawling field. I crept closer to the fence through which she had passed. The fence was crusted orange with rust and the gap narrow—too narrow for a person to pass through it. But big bushes of beautiful white flowers grew at its mouth and all along the base of the old chain link. Surely, Virgo would have crushed them as she'd dragged herself through. Yet, here they sat intact, radiant, absolute and beautiful, as if Heaven itself had touched the earth, and *voila*, there they flourished.

There was no sign of Virgo ever having crawled through the

field at all. I couldn't fit through the gap no matter how I contorted my body, so I climbed the fence. I walked up to the ground where I had seen Virgo laying. The field grew harvest grass with a few flowering stalks intermixed here and there. But right there, where Virgo had collapsed, the land exploded, frantic in deep summer. Full, blooming peonies covered the ground, pregnant in both size and color. Dahlias, with their complicated puzzle of petals, sprouted from the earth, and garden roses hung their heads low as if sleeping off the drunkenness of honey-nectar, waiting to be awoken by the afterglow of sunrise. In the absence of Virgo's body, the ground was thriving and absolutely rich with flora. Rustling, the wind pulled scent away from the flowers, no doubt appeasing honeybees and birds alike.

It made no sense to me. Shouldn't the earth be scorched where a witch like her had lain dead? Suddenly, my stomach sank. What if this was a trap? Perhaps men—lured to this beautiful piece of earth, intoxicated by the scent of fertile flowers—would be wrapped with the arms of the vines and pulled deep into the earth and digested, only to reappear as flora themselves, the ugliness of my own humanity finally turned into something beautiful. I'd be sustaining a source from which goodness could grow.

I leapt back, afraid of what I didn't understand, and made my way back to the safety of my apartment. My body ached, weak from its human transformation. I laid down and lulled off to sleep. I dreamed that I was sitting in a garden with birds cawing above me. A daisy blossom animated next to me. Its body was the length of its stem, and its leaves maneuvered as arms. In one hand, it held a teacup, and it sipped and sipped, but offered me none. How selfish and rude. I wanted tea, too, and I tried to ask for it, but the blossom continued to drink from the cup. Eventually, in anger, I tore the flower straight out of the ground, whereupon it went limp and the teacup shattered on the ground. I lay the flower down, only to discover I had an entire pot of tea sitting in my lap.

For six days, the field exploded in flowers. I watched the small landscape transform through a slit between my curtains. The ground whereupon Virgo had died was dense with summer blooms, their petals expanding out into the world like a deep breath. Passion oranges and fruit-punch reds popped out like fireworks. Seas of royal larkspur and cornflower swayed, pulled in waves by the wind. Birds spent the days hopping around the stronghold of roots, plucking at the worms who were busy turning over the fertile earth. Late in the evening, the frogs would come, slapping their sopping feet against the ground and snapping their sticky tongues at buzzing creatures. Their deep croaking sank into the night, into the dark chorus of evening. Then, the frogs would retreat under the glowing eyes of raccoons and alley cats, ever scavenging, who were only chased away by the dawn chirping of the song thrush belting out his ancient epic. Night and day, the field erupted in this parade of life, with some creatures living and some creatures dying—some who were consumed and others who were nourished by the dead.

On the seventh day, the flowers started to lay low to the ground, resting their stems after a long week of promenading. The birds darted away like show ribbons as the worms tunneled deeper underground and the earth became still. The parade ceased and the field looked like any ordinary patch of land again.

The morning sun had just risen, and the day was placid and quiet. I got out of bed and splashed some water on my face, then dressed. I sat by my window and watched the cars pass on the street outside. The dutiful on their way to work, and the drunks on their way home.

My empty stomach gurgled grotesquely. I hadn't left my apartment in days. I had Virgo's twenty-dollar bills in my wallet, and figured I'd be able to afford a decent meal. It was early enough that my butterfly woman, Maria, would still be on shift.

I glanced at myself in the mirror, ready for Maria to see me whole for once.

I tussled my hair a bit and walked out the door, down the steps, and into the new morning. Across the street, the field lay low and quiet. It had finally finished cycling through whatever magic the witch had done, and the site of it dying down gave me comfort. I had conquered the evil of womanhood, the ugliness that sought to destroy me.

I walked down the street with a swollen chest. Beautiful Maria, who had been so good to me, would see me as a full man. Curse-free, sober, existing in the quiet morning instead of being spit out of the unforgiving belly of night. I couldn't wait to see the smile on Maria's face when she saw me.

I walked into the diner and the bell rang like home. Sweet Maria, with her butterfly eyes and big, pregnant belly—she leaned on the counter, steadying herself with one hand, and the other cradled the small of her back. Her brow furrowed, her eyes closed, and a full tray rested on the counter beside her. She did not look toward the door at the sound of the bell; no one did. All eyes were fixed to Maria as she lifted the heavy tray up to her shoulders. Everyone watched as she carried it down the aisles, serving early-morning men and late-night women. We all stared when she dropped the tray to her side and fluttered back to the counter, and then she finally laid eyes on me.

That smile spread across her face, and she sauntered over to me and took both my hands. "Wow!" she said. "You look almost human!"

I ordered a hearty meal of eggs and steak, a stack of pancakes instead of toast, coffee *and* orange juice. I even asked Maria for a slice of her banana cream pie to go. Talkative, definitive, sober, and with money in my pocket—this was a side of me she had never seen, and she looked at me in disbelief. No one would guess that I had spent the last six days in bed, living off potted meat from the church food bank. Ironic: I had never attended a church service, as I'd never believed there was anything to worship. Eva, on the other hand, had worshiped everything…sunsets and picture frames, puddles that reflected the world back at her.

I felt some of that old pride coming back, that pride that Eva had never understood and which Virgo had attempted to extinguish. Maria was a good woman; I needed someone like her by my side. I promised myself to never seek the company of the sinful again.

Maria served me my food and I ate it all like a rabid dog. She came to clear my plates, and then sat in my booth across from me.

"So," she started, and my chest burst with pride in anticipation of her question, "how did it go with the…?" She cocked her head a little and the sun caught the iridescence of her beautiful wings, and the sparkle of her glittery eyeshadow.

Smirking, I pulled up my sleeves and showed her my clear, un-feathered arms.

Maria grinned. "What did I tell you about that old lady, huh? It's her energy! What did she give you for it?"

I didn't even roll my eyes at Maria's naive explanation for what had occurred. I told Maria all about the small journey I'd had to take, the preparations and attention to detail I'd made, and, of course, finished my story with the slaying of a demon, whose power men would never have to fear again.

Maria nodded, feigning belief in my story. "Maybe now you can slay the demons that women fear," she said.

"Women like you have nothing to fear, Maria," I corrected, smiling into her butterfly face. "You have your husband to protect you, to take care of you, and I can tell that you are a good, honest woman."

She blinked at me.

I cocked my head toward a table in the corner of the room. Lilith sat with two other women in a booth, sequined mini-skirts scratching against the vanilla vinyl, eyes blackened with makeup, fingers still dripping in honey, pollen dusted all over their table. Lilith had no more dominion over me now that I understood what I was capable of.

"But women like them, those women? Those women…they are dangerous."

Maria turned her head toward the women, her mouth slightly agape. One of the women caught Maria's gaze and her striped bee face pulled into a smile, which Maria warmly reciprocated. I frowned.

When her eyes turned back to me, her face turned into a frown, too.

"Cas," she started, "I am a grown woman. I take care of myself." Her hands rested on her round belly. "And there is nothing dangerous about those women; they make their living just like you or me."

Oh, Maria.

"*Maria*," I began, "you make your living in an honest way, but those girls use their bodies to target men. Of course, they're nice to you, but they are *very* dangerous to men."

Maria laughed, a full cackle.

"Cas, we are all out here trying to make a living. All those women are doing is taking advantage of that weakness in a man—the part that wants to conquer, the part that wants to feel powerful over a woman." She winked. "It's not our fault that men underestimate us. Women don't need to be like…like innocent fawns, tip-toeing on newly fallen snow." She put her hands together and held them against her cheek, batting her eyelashes mockingly. "Look at me," she continued, hands circling around her belly, "this ain't no virgin birth!" She laughed at her own joke.

We sat there in silence, her mouth turned into a smile and mine heavy with a frown. Her face now still, her flapping wings slowed and seemed to wither. The color and sparkle of her face began to fade, and she looked more and more human. Her eyebrows lifted suddenly, and she pressed her back against the booth seat. She turned toward the kitchen and called for her husband, but he didn't respond. She turned her legs into the aisle out of the booth, using her arms to steady herself. She looked at me with an unsure face.

"I think it's time," she said.

Maria's husband Anthony rushed out from behind the grill; he was a large, balding man with a handsome face. Kitchen burns scarred his arms and his apron looked like it hadn't been white in years. Maria sat at the edge of the booth, head bowed, taking deep breaths. Anthony, this calamity of a man, was in full panic.

"Come on, Maria," he begged her, "let's get in the car."

Nodding, Maria began to stand, her husband taking her under one arm for support. She stood, took a few steps, and then turned to him with big eyes and whispered, "I'm not going to make it."

His eyes became wide, and he started to plead for her to get into the car. But Maria would take no more steps, and instead, she sat at the edge of another booth, taking both of Anthony's hands into her own as she moaned through contractions.

Anthony looked to the busboy, the only other person he recognized in a diner full of strangers.

The busboy shrugged and said, "I'll go get some towels." He zoomed away into the back, and one of the customers, a man in a red ball cap, got behind the counter and dialed 9-1-1 on a pale yellow, corded phone.

The busboy rushed back with a stack of pink striped towels and laid them out on the floor next to Maria. I got on her right side while Anthony supported her on the left. She stood, and we helped her get down onto the floor so that she could lie down on the towels. Anthony knelt next to her and I crouched on her other side as her face contorted in pain, and she squeezed our hands until they were painful and red.

Lilith wasped over, the two other bees trailing behind. They perched all around Maria, calm and poised. Lilith had Maria's head in her lap, pulling her long hair away from her face. She turned to me and winked. I kept my cool.

Lilith immediately dominated the situation. "Maria, baby," she said, "your body knows the process; you just gotta listen, okay?"

Maria sighed an okay out through her laboring breath.

Lilith got up and crouched next to Anthony, putting a hand on his shoulder as she spoke to Maria. "Okay, baby, we need to get you up on your feet, okay? It's harder to push when you're laying down. We want gravity to help us. Trust me, Maria, baby."

Lilith's voice, for once, was devoid of malice. Maria propped herself up on her elbows. One of the bees corralled all of the customers to the opposite side of the diner, giving Maria some semblance of privacy.

Together, the five of us helped Maria totter up to her feet, and with the guidance of Lilith, she turned toward the booth and grabbed the table for balance. Maria then squatted down low to the floor. She was vocal in her pain, and sweat coated her reddened face. Anthony knelt next to her, bewildered. I stood back with the other two bees, who buzzed, all flushed and glowing.

I shifted from foot to foot and tried to focus my eyes on the window. Satin lines of birds pecked at the window. Butterflies fluttered against the glass. Stray cats lined the bench outside, extending on their hindlegs to see inside. The whole of the natural world brimmed against the aged facade of the Little Midnight Diner.

All the men in the room were in a panic. Where was the ambulance? We needed a goddamned doctor! But the bee women stayed calm, and assured Maria that she was capable, that her body already knew the way.

When it was time to push, I couldn't look away. Maria crouched low, her head resting on her arms—this angel, this mother, and then Lilith, down next to her in her shining patent boots, black ponytail swinging like the devil's tail. Maria pushed and her breath quickened. The bees buzzed around her—hands on her shoulders, slowing down her breathing and quickening the process of birth. With only five intense pushes, Maria's cocoon of a body unfurled into a frantic fluttering of wings, into the shock of life coming into existence. It was a horrible little thing, red and blotchy, screaming for its mother's milk. Lilith caught the baby and immediately pressed it to Maria's chest.

"It's a girl!" Lilith exclaimed.

Anthony beamed at his baby girl, covering her in a towel. Even covered in fabric I could still make out the faint glow of the baby's amethyst heart. The people in the diner clapped, which I didn't understand, as this wasn't a performance. The entire room was a frenzy of noise, birth, pollen, and sequins, and I felt so lightheaded that I practically collapsed into a booth. The wail of an ambulance finally burst from the street. Maria and Anthony knelt together, staring at this living thing that had just come into the world, this absolute bundle of possibility. The door jingled as the paramedics rushed into the diner. Anthony held the baby while the paramedics helped Maria into a wheelchair. Lilith and the other two women headed for the door. The sun was climbing higher, and it was time for their golden-roomed naps. They strutted out of the diner wordlessly, their stilettos tapping furiously against the linoleum floor.

I was so confused. *How is life so possible? How is it so sustained?* I had Virgo on my mind, Virgo whose life I had taken. How was it possible that I was so powerful? I could both create life and extinguish it. Was that even power? People came into the world and left it all the time. I participated in a cycle that began with Adam. Or had it been Cain and Abel?

One woman had died and another had just been born. Virgo's

visceral death; there'd been blood, and then there'd been a body. Similarly, this birth had been so corporeal—no stork, no virgin, and no egg. There'd been blood, and then there'd been a body.

I couldn't understand it.

TWELVE

I used to be in love with this woman, Eva. I really did love her. She lived on the edge of the city, near a set of wild, overgrown train tracks. When we were young, we would steal heavy, brown bottles of malt liquor and walk along those forests that lined the tracks. We poured the liquid into each other's mouths; I'd lick it off her neck. Hiding in the thick, flowered bushes, we kissed; we would make love, and then we'd pass out until the stirring dawn creatures woke us from our drunken stupor.

As we got older, we settled together like dust in the creases of the floorboards. I'd walk through her house as silently as possible, just to get a glimpse of my Eva. I remember one morning when she sat at her kitchen table as still as a doe, eyes just as wide. Her coffee mug lifted to her lips, but she dared not sip; she dared not move a muscle, lest she alert me to where she sat, or who she chose to be that day. I moved around the kitchen slowly, feeling my way around with care, certain not to disrupt the chaos she chose to surround herself in. Clumsily, eyes sealed, I made my way to the chair beside her. Her favorite fragrance was geranium; however, I never told her that I loved her perfume; I would never reveal the pungent clue that always helped me find her without the slightest help from my eyes or ears. For some time, I sat still, eyes closed. I heard nothing except for the air filling her sheer curtains.

With incredible trepidation, I opened my eyes. I sat alone. Geranium blossoms smiled at me smugly from the vase they sat in, living out the remainder of their short lives pridefully.

This woman who I loved, she loved her solitude. The older we got, the less space she kept for me in her cluttered home. Eventually, those loving eyes which always used to look up at me only gazed toward her evergreen couch, her dated wallpaper, and her heavy wooden furniture. She spent her time not with me, but enthralled among her material culture, creating her spaces and her simple paradises, and very seldom leaving them.

That woman, my isolationist. In our youth, we enjoyed the simple life—individual blades of grass, small swaths of lace and other sewing notions, malleable butter that spread over sour bread. Her heart bloomed as full as the bouquets I always brought her. She'd fall in love with all kinds of things, but did she love *me*? She filled her spaces with holy women from religions she found no truth in. She wanted to be devout, as she loved the idea of the devout, but she could only find truth in the erratic cycles of the earth.

Eva fell in love one night after she found a blue sofa in the alley behind her house. One look at that midnight-colored crushed velvet, and it was over; she was in love. Those doe eyes like saucers, her mouth fell open, her hands clasped at her heart. I lugged that thing into her house, and she cried when she saw it in her home. It lived in the attic where Eva painted, and before long, she had painted it, too. She fell in love so often…just not with me.

Eva obsessed over rituals. She spent her mornings feasting. She'd lay out an assortment of pickles and capers, breads, butters, home grown herbs, and bitter greens. She gathered baskets full of hand-ripened fruits—passion fruit, persimmon. She'd eat her fill and then, for good measure, bring out a thick slab of chocolate to soothe her palate. She'd put on these enormous feasts all for herself, and on occasion for me, too. After her meals, she'd carefully repackage everything that had gone uneaten and store it for the next day. She repeated this ritual each morning upon waking, and each day, there would be less and less to indulge in, until six days had passed and she could rest.

After she ate, she'd have a record spinning and recline on the love seat. Her music brought her to tears, so she would lay on the sofa and cry. Sob at nothing, sob at everything, cry because the music instructed her through a subconscious melancholy. She would even cry at the rain…until I reminded her that plants and other living things all need the storms. In life, she felt something rich and deep that I had never before experienced. She was so easily driven to tears by all kinds of things that didn't make sense. She cried once at the sight of a full hydrangea bush, white blossoms covering the ground like a summer snow. She cried at unoccupied porch chairs abandoned on suburban stoops, afraid their owners would miss one beautiful sunset in a calendar full of beautiful sunsets. Sometimes the wind blew a certain way, shimmying the trees, their wild tops twirling in a dance so beautiful that Eva would cry when she couldn't learn the steps.

Her life's work, to calculate how fast she'd have to drive in order to spend her life in constant twilight—this, her great failure. There was nothing, absolutely nothing in this world, that filled her with sadness more than the fleeting sunset. Her favorite time of the day was dusk, but unlike the full day or the depth of night, dusk shifts through rapid successions of color and light, forever fleeing its own existence. Dusk can't be held onto; it can't be savored. In each passing second, time and space is altered. Dusk: the time that brought Eva the most peace, the most satisfaction and imagined purpose in this forsaken life, but it perpetually escaped her.

Despite the heartbreak she experienced each sundown, she immersed herself in night, until I was unable to determine where the night ended and she began. She'd sit there, all midnight and speckled in unconcerned stars, and go through boxes and boxes of her losing lottery tickets. Every time Eva passed a convenience store, she purchased a new ticket. She didn't even want to win—she was afraid to win, afraid to ruin her life with the winnings—but the canons of luck and chance fascinated her.

The pressed ink tickets radiate warmth from their printed genesis. In the moment, and in every moment until the drawing of their lottery, each ticket represents a monument to hope. No one really believes they might win (that they'll admit). But once, each of these tickets was a possible fortune, the difference between poverty and grotesque wealth—the things that money can do, with no thought of what it can't.

Eva said that those who won weren't able to recognize that blessings and curses are one and the same; they both move us around on different paths in this life.

The lottery ticket and its intrinsic magic of improbable hope. The moment the tickets were outed as losers, they turned into garbage, meaningless paper with bright illustrations of lucky charms, and it was that moment which absolutely captivated Eva. She kept her losing lottery tickets in shoe boxes stacked in her closet, wondering if one day they would change their meaningfulness again. She'd lay them out around her, looking for patterns in numbers that had been generated at random—searching for sense, anything with meaning.

I remember Eva mocking the sea with her hips, dancing to the kind of music I'd like to die to…songs that sounded like the end. Some nights, you dance with tears in your eyes. This woman, she always had sunset in her veins.

There were nights when she'd disappear into a state of manic writing, and she would describe this fury of words inside of her, creating worlds that she had to release, agonizing over every single word. Eva would write stories about people flying in airplanes, describing in meticulous detail each person on-board, who they were, and what they wanted. The price of the tickets divided the passengers by class and wealth, with the first class types protected by a champagne silk curtain. Suddenly, the plane turned towards the earth in a protest of its own flight. The plane always crashed in all of her stories. Everyone panics; no one wants to believe that this is their end, until now, life had seemed like forever. They drop to their knees, begging for their lives because this life is all they have ever known, all they can remember.

The fall slows and their panic dulls as their demise is drawn out. They are dying, but what can they do? They try to live their last moments doing worthwhile things, however late that decision may be. The people spend their last moments as carnal, primal beings, returning to animalia. The plane always crashes. Designer handbags tearing into the air, class separation severed as the curtain goes up in flames, the dead resting as unrecognizable human forms.

I would find these stories laid about her desk, intermixed with the occasional, casual suicide note.

I did this to be funny. I promise I was laughing when I did it.
I am so incredibly happy. I'm afraid I'll never be this happy again.
I just wanted to end on a high note.

Then there were Eva's forgotten notes. She left them all around the city for strangers to find. She'd imagine how the finder might derive meaning from her meaningless scribbles, considering it a sign from above, a bit of divine knowledge written on a sticky note. She imagined people taking hold of their lives, thinking someone out there—some omnificent creature—kept an eye out for them. It was just Eva writing nonsense into her notepad.

I remember one summer afternoon and Eva reclined, drunk with a bottle of peach schnapps tilted in the cupholder of our car.

She sped down the road, digging through traffic, unconcerned with safety or living. I remember, in that moment, how nothing mattered. There was no destiny. My life would be forgotten. In that, I found peace. There was no larger plan, no purpose. That meant I could do whatever I wanted. When Eva was gone, I decided to live recklessly, too.

When our inevitable ending finally came, I couldn't take it. Every morning, as if in perfect rhythm with the earth's plates, I would frantically, desperately run to her door, my beating, undulating, hemorrhaging heart pouring from my mouth into my hands, furious and trying to seam everything back together, as imperfect as it was, as much I knew it would all fall apart all over again. I ignored that ominous cracking and creaking in my ear, of a damned foundation, every time; every time, I would pretend that we could be together.

Our families wanted a wedding. I hopped around her yard with a butterfly net and a jar, swatting at the full, iridescent creatures, the big blue eyes on their wings full of laughter at my failed attempts. The one time I actually caught one Eva sank into horror, so frantic to free that dumb butterfly that she didn't talk to me for the rest of the night. When I woke in the morning, I rolled over to my Eva, but instead of her warm body, leathery magnolia leaves filled her indent in the mattress. There would be no wedding, after all.

She wasn't coming back, and it was over; the ground trembled and my feet landed unsteadied, like one leg was longer than the other. Nothing felt *right*, nothing felt *comfortable*. I missed our routines. I had my freedom, but I didn't want it. Freedom unpaced my heart and met me with too many turns, too many wondrous possibilities when all I wanted was what I knew, what I had always known. I hadn't been in love for a long time; neither of us had. I was in love with the familiarity, with always knowing what my day would be. I can't think of a closer conception of Eva's Hell.

After her, I endured a painful rebirth, but I could never get my footing back.

THIRTEEN

I was the Honey Goddess—the goddess of sweetness, love, and tender care. I was a flowering and dying goddess, who sat in both life and death, and distinguished little in between. My love was sacred divination, and my heart dispelled loneliness and the hearts of the troubled. I was Virgo, the cannon of soft pleasure, the ruler of cosmic passion and the pleasure of the Divine.

The night I parted from my mother, she lay in a white bed. A man in a white mask pressed me to my mother's breast. They covered me in a pink blanket. I saw no sky, I knew not of the world or the earth, and I was tired. The night I died, I lay low to the earth and collapsed upon her. A man watched from a second-floor window. Flowers bloomed all over me, covered me, and concealed me from mortal eyes.

In life who was I? What would I be in death? I traveled through the cosmos; I, the speckled stars. I slid down an arc of light, landing in a field, and I lay facing the vastness of a daytime sky. Two large dogs approached me. One was black like forest night, and the other as golden as canyon walls. They trotted to where I lay motionless, blinking up at them. I sat upright and they nuzzled into my shoulders. I stood, and they sauntered away, careening their heads to make sure I followed.

We came to a violet tree, huge and messy, every bloom fluttering in the breeze as if they had tiny wings. One branch ached with the weight of a heavy, glistening fruit, violet blossoms lilting overtop its orange flesh. Butterflies dotted all around the fruit, and the dogs leaped up, but couldn't reach that bending branch. I went up to the tree and plucked the fruit, and the tree groaned with relief, its fatigued branch snapping back up toward the sky.

I held the fruit in my hand and started peeling back the outer layer. Sweet citrus oil burst from the torn skin. The fruit inside was red and blotchy, and squirming. An infant, with all the possibility of the next world, unfurled from the orange shell. She was bleary-eyed, but calm as I peeled off her vessel and held her in my arms.

The dogs trotted back to the arc and I took slow, following steps. I stood next to it, both dogs by my side, baby in my arms, hands anointed with sweet citrus. I crooned to the baby, "You will be the Honey Goddess, the goddess of sweetness, love, and tender care. You will be a flowering and dying goddess who sits in both life and death, and distinguishes little in between. Your love will be sacred divination, and your heart will dispel loneliness and the hearts of the troubled. You will be you, the cannon of soft pleasure, the ruler of cosmic passion and the pleasure of the Divine."

I could see her amethyst heart glowing between her ribs. I placed her on the arc, and she glided away, through the cosmos, into the realm of the living. When she was out of sight, the dogs and I ran through the field, all hazed with the clear sun of spring days.

I remember when I was the egg. No, I was the membranous inside. I lay in the amber yoke, suspended between corporeal existence and not, traveling between the twisting chalazae from the fields of Heaven into the mortal plane. And I came into the world through an act of violence—the breaking of the calcium egg, the tearing through the sustaining membrane of birth. And then I heard my mother's heartbeat from the outside, I suckled the milk, and I was swaddled and rocked to sleep. I know I wasn't the beginning of desire, as desire began with the wail and the breast.

The dogs and I roamed through this paradise until we reached the shores that divided Heaven and Earth. There sat my throne; plush, sapphire upholstery and a frame of golden flowers reaching for the sun because that's all they'd ever known how to do.

I took my place as the silver Queen of Heaven, and oh, how I reclined. The flowers ceased their senseless reaching, and instead they, too, reclined all over me as cape and crown. I gazed into the pool of Earth, watching my first decree unfold. I looked down to the field where my body had lain low. Sure as my flowers bloomed, they died and, one by one, they emerged into the field of Heaven. For that is the deal we make, even though we often forget. When we make our pact with life, we also make a pact with death that we will succumb, and we will return to the earth, we will become it, as our fertility does not end with the womb. We leave our cavernous bodies behind to be eaten by the soil, and the creatures, and the worms, and, yes, here we emerge.

We sat in Heaven's afternoon, bottling the honey of the flowers who bloomed in the afterlife. Ambrosia...we poured it into plastic jugs labeled R*elaxing Milk and Honey Bubble Bath*. Down the arc, we sent it to lowly and destitute places—far away from the hoarding eyes of the wealthy. This was an ambrosia only the downtrodden could afford.

I am Virgo, Queen of Heaven. I am the keeper of the afterlife, where all living things come to rest.

FOURTEEN

Several weeks had passed since Maria gave birth, and I had done little else besides circle job listings in the paper and make the one-block trip to the liquor store. Virgo's field no longer bloomed, and the wilted flowers lay decaying among the worms. I had no desire for whores now, and I had little to occupy my time. My ears barely perked up when I noticed a beautiful woman pass under my window.

The world had long ago revealed to me that there was nothing profound about life. It equated to a series of meaningless events, a list of tasks, that helped us pass the time as we crawled toward our graves. Eva had always been mistaken in her search for meaning, but I'd been envious of the way she would become lost with wonder at the most mundane things. But me, now? I had nothing—certainly not happiness. When I'd had a good job, Eva's two-story home, and a nice car, I had been happy. Hadn't I? How couldn't I have been? My parents had been proud, my father especially so, as I was becoming the kind of man that he had been, stoic, strong, and wealthy. My father had cautioned me all my life not to become too guided by my heart. That's how women are, and they need to be buffered by strong men, he'd said.

If it had not been for Virgo's hyperemotional reaction in the brothel that one summer night, she wouldn't have gotten herself killed.

And I remember how Eva cried so often, and was so weak in the world, so affected by it. But if I'm being honest, I wanted to cry, too. I wanted to feel something deeply, and I wanted to be so moved by the most insignificant things like she was. I wanted to paint like her, I wanted to make art, I wanted to be driven mad by the beauty of the sky. But I was a man. I had to focus on the bigger picture—the house, my car, my climb up the corporate ladder, making a life for us together; Eva stayed stuck in her world where there was no room for me.

But here I was now, shifting through a late August day, and I wanted to feel something. I wanted to experience something profound, and to be just so impacted by the world as Eva had been. I laced up my tennis shoes and headed downstairs. I heard the train whistle in the distance; those trumpets rang out, heralding from the gates of Heaven.

I lingered at the bus stop, but the seashore was only a thirty-five-minute walk. I padded down the street, curious but uninspired. The people I passed wore their grimacing masks against the intense sunlight, and as the day wound lower, the waning sun turned them back into shadows. My shadow was the possibility of me; a beautiful man existing somewhere else, on a different plane. Bending at the world—featureless and black, magnificent. I wished I could dive into his world, into the silence, into a world where the movements of another decided everything I did. How easy would life be if I were bound by the strings of a puppet master…like God, but without His cruelty.

I finally reached the shore, my shadow rippling away into the sand. The velvet sea was a billowing fabric of royal blue drapes flanking a drafty window. The surface was messy with waves, a crushed glass facade concealing an entire internal world brimming with life. I wondered if people were like this, too.

I eased across the seafront, past swarms of bikers and coupled lovers, parents pulling dogs and children close. I walked alone with my shadow. Off the shore, a seaside trapeze school set up their aging apparatus every summer, and I could see people swinging through the air on bars hung with ribbon. I sat at the pier and took off my shoes. My feet dangled in the warm water, a parade of small bright fishes circling around my toes with catches of emerald algae fanning at my arches like silk.

Toward the horizon, the acrobats soared through the air. In their glittering costumes, they looked like birds of paradise, though as the sun continued to set, they, too, became only shadows. A pair dangled from the swinging bar like a woman's crystal earrings and a third dared to jump from a high trapeze, catching the hanging shadow by the wrist, a fish caught at sea.

The clouds sat low in the sky, full and ruffled like my feathers had once been. They sat thick and clustered together like a throne. I imagined the angels sitting up and down its arms, perched and feathered, entranced with the cirque just like I was. Light pierced through the nebula, rays of golden light that cut through the water miles ahead, where the still sea lay like the crisp sheets of a freshly made bed. Out there, the water only rippled under the feet of a settling bird, or over the mouths of feeding fish. While it lay undisturbed, it breathed like a great earthly lung.

My Eva had found the sea to be so beautiful. How cliché of her—who didn't find the sea beautiful? Only every artist who'd ever lived had found its sapphire stretch and crystal sands poetic. And yes, it was beautiful. The light did special things at the seashore, things that it didn't do inland.

The sun kept setting in its bloody orange way, and I stared at this bergamot death of a day. Night rushed in, ushering in its world. The blackened horizon looked like the apocalypse, a hypnotic black line facing an entire civilization that was oblivious to its presence every night. The shadows of other people had turned away from the blackened sea, and instead they beamed at the brightly lit city of glass that illuminated the night and drowned the stars right out of the sky. Here, they gazed at their creation, their own species' ingenuity, and thanked their gods that they had been delivered from the wildness of the natural world. Inside their cities, they remained safe from the black depths of the horizon.

In a city, there is nothing to fear from the dark but each other.

I wished I could reach that impossible line and fold myself into the dimension that it opened into. What would it mean to crawl deeply inside of the night, and not only be overcome by it every sunset? I took shallow steps into the tide, wanting no part of the city or this society we called *civilized*. This city, its inception, built by humans in chains, continued to entangle personhood with inescapable norms and constructs.

Rolling up the hems of my pants, I walked as far out as I could without getting them wet; I was no rebel. Thick storm clouds crowded into the sky, and the wind wound steadily. The air smelled like brine and stung as the wind whipped sand across my face. With a pit of sadness, I watched the gray clouds cover the black line of horizon. Shatters of lightning split through the glowing overcast. They lay against the sky, patterned like the veins pressed into my arms by God himself—His own simple routine. There was no following of thunder, so the storm surely raged miles away.

I headed back to the shore, unsatisfied with how deep I'd been able to go without getting my pants wet, and headed toward a jetty that strutted right out toward that pitch black universe of sea. The spring had been exceptionally wet, and the waters had shrunk the beach by several feet. The jetty sat completely submerged near the shore, and I had to trudge through calf-deep water in order to follow the path out to sea. The water lessened as the jetty's elevation rose. Black waves lapped up over my feet before retreating into the velvet billows of the ocean. The damp cement was slippery with a film of green scum that had grown and thrived all over the newly submerged jetty. I kept my footsteps careful and steady.

The wind was picking up more furiously now, and the black waters followed suit. I was afraid to continue, afraid that I would be dragged into the sea and pulverized against the steel beams of the jetty. I turned back toward the city, the line of artificial light that made darkness and solitude impossible. I couldn't go back. That black horizon called to me like a siren.

The wind was manic, and so was I. My steps were much less careful now, and I slipped and slid through the algae, through the slapping waves—trying to run, but all I could do was stumble. I lost my footing and fell hard onto a knee, my hands scraping against the concrete. My pants and flannel sleeves soaked up saltwater. I righted myself and again tried to run, but this time, I fell face-first onto my elbows. So, I crawled down that jetty, desperate to crawl into that black horizon. I ignored the aching protest of my knees and the sting of my palms.

When I had almost reached the end of the jetty, I managed to stand, and I took those last careful steps to the portentous edge. The concrete ended in an unforgiving drop into the sea. The transition from stable platform to open water was almost impossible to see through the black ocean. The tide slammed up against the jetty, forceful and loud. As the tide pulled back, the water sucked down deep, exposing the corroded metal platform that held up this concrete slab. That evil undulation hissed like a pit of snakes, bubbling and foaming like a chemist's reaction. The ocean raged wildly against this man-made intrusion into its skin, working to take it into its body and consume it, as the ocean had consumed so many things.

The water rolled—black glass candy pulling through a mill, the white moon exposing the jagged crests and troughs of each wave. Black night was all around me, and this intense desire to be absolutely consumed came over me. It was a desire I couldn't understand, and it seemed not to come from me, but some invisible external force. Fear gripped at all of my senses. The water was frantic, and I was far out from shore. The water could easily overtake me, but I *wanted* to be overtaken. Didn't I? If I could get away from the jetty, out into those black rolls, I would surely be able to float along in their folds, and then swim back to shore. *I would not die. I want to feel something.*

The sky blinked with a million stars, little eyes all watching to see what I would do next. I took several, full-legged steps backwards. I started forward, but the squeaking of my soggy shoes stopped me. I took off my shoes, my socks, my soaking pants, my damp button-down, and my undershirt, too. A few leftover feathers rustled out of sleeves and were pulled out to sea. I looked around sheepishly, but there was no one on the shore who I could see. I was a naked man, a city dweller, out on a black pier trying to fulfill some inane primal desires I'd convinced myself I still retained.

I began to sprint, though my gait was awkward as I tried to steady myself against the slick surface. I gained a meager velocity, but still, I jumped off the very edge of the jetty, and for one glorious moment, I was in that black horizon, cruising straight through that mysterious line. I splintered into the water, arms and legs flailing, and sank down into the brine of the ocean, where I waited for the buoyancy of my body to lift me back through that undulating line that divided my world from this one. But my body kept sinking—slowly but steadily, I sank further away from those gazing stars. I kicked my legs hard and pushed through the water with my arms; I wrestled with this tremendous aquatic force that swirled around my every limb.

The water pulled down at my legs, but I struggled against its hold. I became as frantic as the cresting ocean itself as I fought my way up to open air. Finally, I broke through the suffocating membrane and sucked in a huge breath. In the seconds that I'd been plunged underwater, the rain had arrived in a deluge. The ocean water was insane and impossible to navigate. I flailed toward the shore, desperate for land. A shadow stood at the edge of the jetty—someone who hadn't been there when I'd jumped, I was sure. I yelled out to them for help in between mouthfuls of brine, but they remained motionless as they watched me struggle.

Suddenly, the waters began to hollow where I struggled to stay afloat, and walls of waves started to crawl up around me. I sank lower into the hollow, the wall of sea completely encasing me. My heart in my stomach, I prayed to the Divine of the lowly for salvation, but it was in vain. To my horror, the walls began to cave in, crashing on top of me and pushing me down like huge hands, pummeling me into the sea as if they were fists.

I made one final call out to the lithe figure on the jetty. The clouds angled the moonlight so that it illuminated the jetty just enough for me to make out an unmistakable woman.

"Your debt has been paid!" Lilith called out to me.

And I sank deep into my watery grave.

FIFTEEN

I was Cassius, a dry land man. Now, I am a shadow at the bottom of a saltwater prison. In life, I drew out stark boundaries for my own manhood and wouldn't dare to be affected by the world around me. I was interested only in what was profitable, or powerful, or walked around on lithe legs and thick hips. I wouldn't allow myself to cry at beautiful things; I wouldn't allow myself to cry at things that moved me. I loved a woman who loved me, but who didn't want to be captured by the society that I so firmly rested my identity on, and so she went away. I questioned why she left, why everything that everyone had told me my entire life I should want couldn't be enough for her. I threw it all away, but she didn't come back. So, I consumed women, I wantonly disregarded the sacred, and I was so often empty; just one time, I felt powerful.

A Goddess submerged me deep into the sea. My waterlogged lungs were relieved only when I sank far underwater, out of view of the stars, of humanity—my own, as well as that which crawled across the earth.

The floor of the ocean is alien except for bottle caps and fishing nets. I once found the dazzling treasure of a lost wedding ring. It was engraved with, *I just can't do it.* There are other men here, too—us, a special heard of those dumb enough to disregard the inherent divinity within women. We wander along the murky bottom, disrupting schools of fish, overturning settled shells. We cannot tell each other our stories, as we cannot speak. We are primitive men, naked and grunting, nomads with no destination, hunting out of boredom instead of need.

But I am fulfilled. It is wondrous to live in such an intense mystery, with absolutely no knowledge of the world above. I draw in the sand, and no one has the words to judge me. We cry out lifetimes of tears in silence, raising sea levels drop by drop. Here, everything sways as if dancing to a forever samba. We sway, too—eyes closed, hands up in surrender—we sway to the dark silence underneath the sea.

THE STORY OF EVA

ONE

On some idle summer night, Cas and I sat in the drive-thru of our local fast food joint. The restaurant sat on a black stretch of road, and the people inside wandered through the fluorescent lights, hustling from station to station as if they were manning a spaceship. Outside, we drowned in the neon beams shooting out from the window signs.

A man was mingling amongst the cars, hands first raised in prayer and then extended as he begged for change. As he approached us, the car in front of us pulled forward. We told him we had no money, then drove up to the window to pay for our food. Cas looked in the rearview window, back at the man.

"What if that guy is really God?" he asked.

We drove home with greasy fingers and salt dried palates. I couldn't shake the image of the man, and I replayed in my mind how his hollow cheeks had been sunken in with hunger, and how we had pulled away from him, laps warmed with our paper bags full of food. From the depths of my guilt, not concern for the man's wellbeing, I convinced Cas to drive the short distance back to the restaurant so we could feed the man.

Annoyed with me as always, Cas obliged. We pulled back into the drive-thru, but the man wasn't there, which made Cas angry, so I got out of the car and went inside. The woman at the counter smiled a warm smile that was rare at this time of night. I asked her about the man. She told me that she knew who I was talking about, and he wasn't supposed to be out there, but that she would never stop a man from trying to get fed. She explained how, on some early mornings, there would be a lot of extra from the night before, and she would bring it to the nearby park where the man slept. I ordered him a cheeseburger with extra fries, and the woman slipped in a few other extras as well.

I got back into the car.

Cas didn't want to go to the park. He was angry that I'd made him drive back to the restaurant for some *crackhead*. We parked the car in front of our apartment building and he walked up the stoop while I got into the driver's seat.

"Where are you going?!" he yelled.

"Where do you think?"

Furious, he got into the car, complaining the entire way back.

"You didn't have to come with me," I told him, rolling my eyes.

When we reached the park, we saw the man seated on a bench muttering to himself. I walked towards him, Cas like an anchor at my side. The man didn't look towards the sound of our footprints.

"Hi," I said, "were you at the burger place earlier? In the drive-thru?" The man looked suspicious, or confused. "I'm not sure if it was you," I told him, "it was dark."

Cas stood behind me silently.

"We just wondered…"

The man looked up at me, and I lost all of my words.

"Wondered what?" he asked.

"We wondered if you were…if you could be…God."

I'd laughed as the words tumbled out, shaking my head.

I shook myself into my senses, Cas shifting from foot to foot behind me. "I'm sorry," I said. "This is ridiculous." I handed him the food and started to turn away, but the man touched a few fingers to my swinging wrist.

He sat on the park bench in tattered clothes, arms down his sides, legs spread.

"I don't know how you knew," He said in a deep, croaking voice. "I am God."

My jaw dropped, and my heart welled. Eyes widened, I grasped Cas' hand to steady the quake of a human body confronted by its very creator. I dropped to my knees and pulled Cas down with me. He scowled and squirmed his hand away from mine, but knelt all the less.

"Hello, God," I said.

"My children," God said, "get up and sit with me."

We stood and took our places on the bench with God. He looked into my eyes as He took a swig from a paper-bagged bottle. I took His face in my hands, running my thumbs over coarse facial hair and streaks of dirt. Full tears fell from my eyes as I mustered my plea to the King of Heaven and Earth, He who'd imagined everything that was, all of existence residing within Him—the entire universe and all its inhabitants; the inventor of love, hate, and war, and the keeper of our destinies and the meaning of life itself.

"God," I whispered, "what is it that we need to do?"

After another long swig, God replied.

"The world is ending. Go get all the money you have and bring it to me, your God." He ended his thought with a smirky laugh.

Again, I knelt and I took his hands into mine.

"Okay," I promised, and I turned to Cas, his sour face and eyebrows furrowed at me. I stood, now taking Cas' hands into mine and pulling him up and into me.

"Eva," he started.

"No, Cas. Let's go."

He followed me back to the car silently. We had barely climbed inside before he started with his lecture.

"Eva, that guy is drunk. What were you thinking?"

I turned to him, absolutely astonished, with tears running paths down my cheeks. "Jesus, Cas! God Himself tells you the world is ending, and all you care about is the fact that he's a drunk?!"

And thus began our epic fight, the infamous brawl that ended our romance once and for all. I sat through several minutes of Cas calling me a lunatic, a psycho, and naïve and dramatic, attention-seeking—anything he could think to throw at me. He yelled all about how I couldn't take care of myself, how I needed him, how much I would be lost in life without him. This coming from the man who had lived in my home all these years because he had nowhere else to go.

It was hard for me to argue with Cas. He was too aggressive and domineering, too unwilling to consider my side of reality. During every fight we ever had, I would sit in silence and soak up all of his anger. Then, I would write him pages and pages of letters, explaining everything he had said and how exactly he was wrong, as well as how he always completely missed the point of the argument.

I must have written him hundreds of letters.

This time, there was no time for a letter, the world was ending. So, when Cas slowed to a stop at the next red light, I jumped out of the passenger's side and ran straight into the woods.

"Eva, what the fuck are you doing?!" echoed behind me. I heard the slam of a car door, and chasing footsteps. I ran through the dark until I reached a low-branched tree. I climbed until I felt consumed by the black canopies. Cas stood at the edge of the forest, calling for me and cursing me to hell.

After several minutes, he gave up. He got back in the car and left me alone in the forest. I climbed down, and my feet found their way onto trails that I had walked for years, trails my body knew like an ancestral line. Eventually, I made my way through the trees and into my own backyard. I looked around at my living trees, with bundles of nesting birds tied together in the branches. The world was ending, but how could they know?

I touched a hand to the bark, and it touched back like rough skin. What would a tree do if it knew the world was ending? Would it thrust down its roots, gripping the soil and the roots of other trees to resist the inevitable? I imagined the trees passing notes between their root systems, all around to their families and neighboring trees. Maybe they'd hold their heavy limbs closer, cradling all of the living things that had called their branches home for the entirety of the tree's life, and succumb to rest in a world that no longer would be.

How beautiful my garden had grown during my life. All of the very small lives that lasted just a season had brought me more joy than many lives that lasted much longer. Teary and trembling, I walked through my weedy garden and up my backsteps. As I stepped inside my home, I heard the crack of tires over gravel as the headlights of a car filled my front room's windows. I pushed a heavy wooden cabinet in front of the back door, then ran to the front and slid the chain lock secure.

I flew up the stairs to my bedroom just as Cas' fists began a rhythmic beating of my front door. I heard him screaming through the space in the door that the chain lock allowed, faintly, from the floor down below, but Cas' time was up. And so was mine; the world was ending, and God had not been uncertain in his instructions. I flung open my closet doors and began to hurl Cas's clothes out of an open window. Cas filled this quiet night with shrieks and curses and begging. But all I could hear was the woosh of his airborne clothes, and the sound of my broken chains as they hulked to the ground and curled like snakes around my feet.

I pulled money out of drawers, books, pillows, floorboards,

cans, and coffee cups. I'd stored my life savings like a squirrel burying nuts for the winter. I'd only put away five dollars here, ten dollars there, but piling it all up on my kitchen table, I realized I had saved up a lot of money. What did I ever care about money? I had my home. What else did I need?

I had this home, my beautiful home that would not survive the end of the world. I looked around at all of my possessions—books, photographs, paintings, plants, seashells, silk scarves, and treasures of every kind. This home was a museum documenting my life and everything I had loved. I had kept and curated so many things, and written manuscript after manuscript, so that my child would grow up in a home of wonder, and so that when I was gone from the Earth, she would have all these veins of me to try to understand me through. I didn't want to be remembered by the world, but through a single like line, a child.

I'd never told Cas that I wanted a family, as I didn't want the family with him. I'd dreamed of growing a girl in my garden, being a mother of immaculate conception. Just me and my baby, our little team. Cas hung on my ankles like shackles, and a baby meant a life sentence with him. It frightened me to give up my freedom and independence so irreparably, with such permanence. For my *tocaya* and only her, I would settle down. I imagined her running through my house, fist-fulls of glitter thrown in the air, ransacking my closets full of sequined clothes and oversized costume jewelry. I'd let her paint on anything she wanted, creating her own masterpieces within my home. Eva's daughter, up in the trees, eyes towards the sky. Here on earth, yes, but not quite.

My heart now ached at this dream that would go unrealized. My home, my garden, all the beautiful things I had collected in shoeboxes and satin bags, would be destroyed. I'd, of course, known I would one day die, but I'd always believed my things would long remain to tell the story of me. Now, I imagined the entire planet exploding, charred pages full of my handwriting floating into orbit.

I peered out the window and watched Cas balling up his possessions and throwing them into the back seat of his car. I opened the window a crack and screamed, "THE WORLD IS ENDING—WHY ARE YOU WASTING YOUR TIME?" Before he had the time to reply, I slammed the window shut, just as heaving sobs rose up from my core and spilled out into an ending world. Cas could not see the guardian angels peering at him through muddy puddles. He could not hear the heralding trumpet of the whistling train, calling floods of angels into Heaven every day; animals and plants and every organism, pulled into streams of light pooling from vascular clouds, every one of them crooning, "Now is my time." He just couldn't see it. A velvet blue couch, losing lotto tickets, the forever fleeting sunset.

I wept as I said goodbye to my beautiful home.

"I will meet you in the ether of things, I suppose."

Slipping out the back door with Cas still red-fisted at the front, I made my way back into the woods, a backpack full of my life's savings slung over my shoulder.

TWO

The forest floor was mud, and I quickly lost my sandals. My barefoot feet were black with soil climbing up my ankles, leaves twisting themselves into my hair. I emerged onto the road and found myself under the fluorescent glow of the restaurant. Walking to the bench where I had first encountered God, I trembled. He lay prostrate on the bench, a humbled God. His arm draped to the cement ground, his fingers resting against a brown paper bag wrapped around a bottle, a pungent liquid spilling from its mouth.

I shook him awake, as there was no time. He startled out of sleep, pushed himself up onto his forearms, and turned to me with wild eyes.

"I'm just sleeping here! What's it to you? I'll be gone by the God-damned morning!"

I didn't understand his anger towards me. "God?" I whispered.

"Oh," he said, "you're back."

I sat the backpack on the ground and unzipped it. I began to pull out wads of cash, and his eyes popped out of his skull.

I knelt and placed the cash at his feet, and he didn't hesitate to scoop it up and plunge the bills deep into his pockets. He grinned a huge grin and shook his head. "I can't believe it," he said.

I didn't understand.

"Trust me, sweetheart, one day you'll thank me for this. You're free now, and no one will know you by all the precious things you keep!"

He was laughing now, as he gathered up all of his belongings and practically sprinted away.

"Thank you!" he called back. "Thank you!"

I stood alone, the paper-wrapped bottle at my feet. What had just happened? God and all of his humanness there with me on Earth one moment, and then he was gone. I looked around and waited for something to happen; waited for the Earth to open up and swallow me whole, or for the moon to fall straight out of the sky and crush me and everything living. There was nothing. It was late August, and the only sounds were the creaking of deep summer, the vespers of the last nights before the dying season.

Dawn was beginning to flood into the sky, and I wondered to myself, *What is the most beautiful thing I have ever known?* Across the street, there was an abandoned garden in which someone had planted fruit trees decades ago. They'd only in recent years begun to yield harvests. The place was a wild paradise in its own shaggy way. Sometimes when we went through the drive-thru, Cas and I would lay out a blanket and eat in the middle of the garden. Against a petal-pink sky, I crossed to say goodbye to this weedy place.

Crickets were slowing their night chorus; I could see them sitting in the heads of tulips, their petals splayed out like burst hearts. I had passion for the garden—eating the sweetest fruits, inhaling the fragrant flowers, and remembering Cas's soft lips against my neck. I looked around at everything that grew. An apple tree bent heavy with fruit rooted itself against a splaying wood fence, mangled by the growth of the tree.

Looking out into this placid world, I started to realize that the world was not ending. But who lies about being God? Only all of the men throughout history, I guess. The kings and queens with their divine monarchies, the colonizers and their manifest destinies. They must think themselves God to act with no fear of His judgment. God was not someone I prayed to; I prayed to much smaller things. I had wanted the world to end, so I'd believed that it would.

Mine was already ending.

I was so hungry. I picked apples from the tree, but I had no appetite to eat them. I put them in my backpack. So, the world wasn't ending. But I had ended things with Cas—something I had wanted to do for so long. Too little, too late, unfortunately. It was too late for me, as my world was ending. I saw only two choices; I could either kill myself, or let my world end. But I didn't want to die and forsake a world as beautiful as this.

I felt so stupid. I had an appointment that coming morning at the women's clinic, but I'd just given away all the money I had, my sacrifice to God, and now I had no money to pay for the procedure. I started making my way home as all of the songbirds were starting to wake up in a world that had not ended, and they sang out their sacred praise for another day on Earth.

THREE

I walked home along the road. Coming to my front door, I found Cas's car still parked outside and Cas asleep in the driver's seat. I knew he had nowhere to go, but he'd never considered my house a home anyway. I ascended my wooden stairs with soft feet, afraid to wake Cas and plunge us back into an altercation; or worse, I feared that we would make up.

I wandered into my kitchen, flecks of dried mud dusting from my ankles and all over my floor. I was happy to be home, in my beautiful space, and finally alone. I opened the fridge several times, my appetite still refusing to let me eat. I usually loved to eat—loved to open beautifully packaged foods and place them onto beautifully detailed serving plates. Meals had always been central to my family growing up, and my mother would make a splendour out of every supper even though it was just us. So, every morning, I would make myself small feasts, celebrating the beginning of another day.

Cas had never understood the importance of ritual. For him, it was a piece of toast and he was out the door. I hated that. Rituals are what connect us to who came before us, our indoctrination into what is sacred. Cas criticized them as being mindless—asking, *If we don't know why we do something, why should we keep doing it just because it's tradition?* But Cas didn't understand. The religious don't eat pork because God commanded this be so. We don't remember that pork was dangerous to eat, and that those who abstained from the meat distinguished themselves from idolaters. True, too, is it for the birds, who fly south every winter because God commanded it. They're too far removed to remember the deadly winters that would overcome those birds who chose to disobey. Our rituals come from challenges in life that those before us encountered, and my rituals come from my own struggles, which I was determined not to repeat.

I looked out my kitchen windows, which faced the yard. I gazed at all of the beautiful things that would live for a season and die. I was so much like them. Yes, I lived season after season, but with each new iteration of spring, I was born again. My body, too, would come into spring like returning to a lover from long ago. Those vernal hands, damp with rain and warm from sun, would hold my breasts, larger now and striped with stretch marks; those hands would cover my softening belly and filling hips.

"Is that you, Eva?"

And it was! It was me! But through those dark, frozen months, I swore I had died my yearly death, just like the world around me. The bare tree branches stretched through hibernal evening skies like the veins in my arms. But then the old trees came budding, and they began to conduct their great symphony of spring. And every season, I was reminded that the earth is always alive just under the surface, the surging of worms and roots under a warm soil. As the trees flowered, I, too, realized, *Here I am, always just beneath the surface, ready to come into bloom when it is my season.* Those rainy days I despised so much were so necessary for all the things to grow.

My yard trees, my old friends. Fall was coming quickly and

all their leaves would fall. The season of my life was coming to an end. I stepped out into my backyard and rustled through the grass with my bare, muddy toes. I chose a shaded patch of wildflowers in a corner of the yard. The sun would pass over them as the day drew longer, but for now, they remained cool and covered by the very early morning. I stepped carefully into the growth and lay under the bush. From where I lay, I could see a little white and orange cat, nibbling through the overgrown grass. I could hear my neighbor, a beautiful curly haired woman, watering her garden next door. The backdoor of her home creaked open, and I heard her animated husband explaining all about how he had won $1600 from a poker tournament he had played all night in the next city.

When they went inside, I closed my eyes. I would lay here until death took me, and the flowers in my garden would grow through me, cover me, and consume me. Then I would be reborn, season after season, through them.

"What are you doing?" a voice asked curiously.

I opened my eyes. The sun had long passed overhead and was beginning its western descent. I had slept the entire day away.

"What are you doing?" a woman repeated.

I sat up, my shoulders pushing the flower bushes to either side of me. I blinked at this woman, an old woman with long white hair who wore a tattered bathrobe in the heat of an August afternoon. She was standing in the alley, her face pressed through a gap in my picket fence.

"N-nothing," I stuttered, "I'm not doing anything. I was asleep."

The woman smirked. "And do you always sleep in the dirt?"

I met her curiosity with a frown. "No," I said.

"Well then, why today?" she asked.

I pulled my knees up to my chest and inhaled deeply, rolling my eyes. "Well, if you have to know, I am waiting to die."

"Waiting to die?!" she asked incredulously. "Well, how long is that going to take?"

I maintained my frown. "I don't know. Hopefully, not too long."

The woman looked around until she found my back gate. She let herself in without asking, and crouched down beside me with a surprising dexterity.

"And are you going to take the baby with you?" she asked, motioning to my stomach.

My heart dropped.

I looked at her with huge eyes. "How do you know?!"

"I know things," was her only explanation. "Now, tell me, child, what's going on here?"

And perhaps it was because I felt so very alone despite this fetus in my belly, but I chose to confide in this very strange woman who'd been spying on me from the alley.

"I am not ready to be a mother," I told her. "And this child would bind me to this man forever, and that would be an intolerable fate."

God, I was so young. My mother had given birth to me at forty, after many, many seasons of independence and adventure. It was impossible that this was my time.

"I see," said the woman. "But why kill yourself, my dear? Surely, there are other options." I explained how I had been naive, and had been scammed out of all my money on the morning of my scheduled abortion.

"I wanted to believe he was God because it was a relief to think that someone had all of the answers. It's difficult to figure life out on my own."

"And how do you know that he was not God, dear?" she asked inanely.

"Because the world did not end. And why would God want

money? What's money to the creator of creation?"

The woman scoffed. "The world did not end, and yet here you are laying under a bush waiting to die. Something is indeed ending for you, my dear. You have no more money, so that's an end; your lover's entire possessions are out of your house and in his car, and that's an end. You want to die, my dear, then let us die," she ended with a warm smile.

A pang of fear shot through me. Had this woman been watching me all night? But I was going to kill myself anyway, so what could she possibly do to me?

"How should I do it?" I asked in a whisper.

"Eva, my dear…."

I had not told her my name.

"You are a sacred thing, a divinity in the world. Without this form, you can wander through this world without inhibition; hide out in the threshold until you are new again. Your child can be made anew, too."

I blinked at this woman and her beautiful words of indecipherable meanings. Whatever it was, I wanted it, and adventure in the heart of death gave me a chance at freedom.

"Sign me up," I told her.

The woman sprang up and out the back gate. I stood up and peered over the fence. She rifled through a shopping cart teetering with things. Coming back into the yard, she laid out a dark blue crochet blanket.

"Eva, you are aware of the sacred, so here you will lay in this ocean."

Into the ocean, I lay. She fished around in the deep pockets of her bathrobe and pulled out a clear, plastic bear filled with honey. The liquid was amber and unblemished. Kneeling over me, the woman lifted my shirt and squirted the entire bottle onto my stomach. It was warm from being inside her pocket on such a hot day. She took both of my wrists in her hands and directed my palms right into the honey. With her bony fingers guiding mine, I rubbed the honey all over the slight mound of my belly and down my curving sides.

The woman stood and surveyed my yard. She plucked a handful of wilting flowers, and shook their heads over my stomach until it glittered with pollen.

She said, "You are Eva, a primordial spirit of the earth, wild soil, and, in life, the unyielding seed. Your life is of the brightest joy, of color, of music, of explosions. Around every turn for you awaits wonder, your heart rhapsodic and wild as marshes and jungles and all free places."

I breathed in deep and let this unknown magic encapsulate me like an insect in amber. Again, the woman stood, and she plucked a sunset orange persimmon from my old tree. Kneeling by my head, she lifted my shoulders into her lap. With a small paring knife which she produced out of her bathrobe, she carved up the fruit and fed me slices. My appetite had returned and I was ravenous. The woman plucked five or six more fruits before I was satiated. I lay in her lap and she caressed my hair like a mother. Her fingers gently touched the gold chain that strung my pendant. I watched as the pollen flecks grew and transformed into the smallest-petaled flowers I had ever seen. After some time, she took a paint-stained putty knife and scraped the crusting honey off of my skin, and then she carefully rebottled it, flowers and all.

"I know the perfect home for your child, the daughter of Eva. They will nurture her until you return."

"Where am I going?" I asked.

The woman did not answer. She was busy wiping the honey from my palms.

"Why is it that all the things that are freeing to a woman are considered sins?" she asked. "Be sinful, my Eva, and eat the apple. Whatever is wrong with a little sin?"

FOUR

I ate the apple and I fell into sweet yellow dreams with a southern sun, impossible waters, low notes, and the crystal music of shattered glass. A life alone with me only, my truest love.

I remember sailing on a train through the black sky like a diamond bracelet. I left the earth and floated through space and time like sewn lace. I found freedom in this wondrous constellation of glittering stars, each a poked hole in an endless black sky, from which the inhabitants of Heaven could observe a paradise squandered. My simplest paradise, and I, swirled through time past a beloved black dog curled up in a forgotten summer, the simplicity of dying and the natural passing of time, past a plowed field waiting to become wild again.

Deep inside of soil, I was roots, reaching and feeling in between the mortal and the everlasting, lost within the ceaseless transitory nature of becoming humus and then becoming alive again. I was an amaranthine soul becoming and becoming again. At times, I shrank down to impossible sizes and lounged on blades of grass, wetting my palate with drops of rain. Once, I watched a frantic beetle scurrying back towards his nesting fellows, panting and bewildered.

"My friends!" he exclaimed. "You won't believe what just happened to me!"

The other beetles scurried up to him, clearly intrigued by this bit of beetle gossip.

"I was collecting roots and seeds," he said—and this was only partly true, as I had seen him with my own eyes attempting to court a rather disinterested female beetle—"minding my own business," he continued, "when, out of nowhere, this MASSIVE apparition fell out of the sky and almost crushed me!" The massive apparition had been the foot of a jogger who was absolutely unaware of the beetle, nor his desire to mate. "It was THIS close to killing me!" And he held his small beetle hands close together to illustrate the near miss. "I almost died," he continued. "Died! It is a miracle I am alive—God has given me another chance!"

The other beetles were quite disinterested by this revelation and began to wander towards the core of an apple strewn in the grass.

"I must have a higher purpose in this world!" he cried to deaf ears. Though, I heard him, and I believed it to be true.

I continued on through sites of depravity, the stages of human violence, wars, massacres, and genocides. The blood of the dead had made the soil rich, and plants and animals had taken over these human-built places. The plants photosynthesized and the animals raised their young, completely unaware of what had occured on the land which they made their lives. These creatures, just like the Divine, were not ashamed of their bodies, or fertile blood. The Divine bowed for the beautiful Calathea, in wonder of the glory of its own creation. And the beautiful Calathea did not rustle its foliage smugly in the face of the Divine, no. It, too, bowed for it, understanding that its own creation was just a chance—its life a mere condition, and its mortality an ancient inevitability

Many years into my journey, the world began to flood. The

glaciers melted and the living floated up closer and closer to the sky. We became a people of the clouds, the sea ever below our feet, and a thin stripe of sky just above us. It was a wonderful existence, floating in the ocean water that beat like a heart, reaching up to caress the foam of clouds. One day, I curled into a cottony cumulous and fell fast asleep. I awoke to nightfall, though the moon was covered. I heard what I thought was the sound of running water, but when I opened my eyes, I saw it was the rustle of trees in the wind. I wasn't in the clouds, but in the heart of a meadow, lying on dry, solid land. I worried it might have all been an elaborate dream, but my leg burned with a jellyfish sting that laced like a rosary around my ankle.

Two dogs walked towards me: earthly guardians of the field, and in the threshold of death, guardians of the living. I peered down onto the Earth and saw what looked like a meteorite streaking down towards the planet. The ocean below sank deep and hollow, and that's when I saw him. It was Cas.

In my hidden place, I had waited, watching the world with wondrous eyes; the phosphorescent glow of humanity burning out, the divine beings in condemned places, and the silken darkness of the natural, untouched world at night. Now there was a beginning, it was only a thread pulling across time. I returned to the Earth like a long awaited spring. I unfurled like all living things after a long sleep. I poured down upon the wild earth; I gave dying things life again. I was a lilac breeze searching through the depths of night. I came back and houseplants overtook their homes, paved ways were ruined by the long-awaiting roots of things wanting to grow, and berries grew so full that they burst off the vine, coloring the earth aubergine and crimson.

Here, in this earth, I can be a woman without a man, and I, too, am bursting

I woke up and I was. I had dreamt of an enormous water goddess who stepped canyons into the earth, and filled oceans and rivers into the craters where she had lain. When I opened my eyes, it was so. There was a paradise in the earth, and I was the first to see that this is *beautiful*. I remember thrusting my hands into the soil, filling my palms with paradise. Microscopic things caressed my skin, invisible in the black mother of all earthly things.

I stood on the interstate, stars falling all through my life. I am Eva, a primordial spirit of the earth, wild soil, and, in life, the unyielding seed. I will create my life as a soft parade, the brightest of joy, of color, of music, and explosions. Around every turn lies wonder, and my heart beats, rhapsodic and wild as marshes and jungles and all free places.

THE END

Emiliana Helfeld has an academic background in Anthropology. For five years Helfeld worked at the front desk of a strip club, which largely influenced her perception of the human condition as well as the content of her fiction. She loves animals, dancing, and spectacle.

Connect with Emiliana on Instagram: @Emiliana.333

Made in the USA
Monee, IL
18 July 2021